NOTHING EXISTED, BUT THE TWO OF THEM.

They were set apart in a world where awareness meshed with need and flamed into a raging inferno between them.

Cory's breath, labored from the exertion of dancing, fanned her neck as he pulled her to him. Then he was kissing her, their lips meeting in a renewal of the slow motion dance begun earlier in jest.

It was a kiss that shifted and swayed–that held, released, and held again.

His touch was exquisitely tender. One hand supported her weight while the other cupped her chin. Gentle fingers roamed the hills and valleys of her face in a timeless rhythm.

So sweet.

So perfect.

So right.

What about Krystal? The unwelcome thought intruded itself on Nance's passion-tinged awareness. She drew back in halfhearted protest.

Cory responded by pulling her even closer to him. She was encompassed by the heat of him, by the spicy scent of his cologne. She was teased by a surging swirl of emotion that bid her to put away reason.

Unable to resist, she surrendered to the sweet tumult of passion. Abandoning the last ties of sanity, casting off the last of clinging reserve, she lifted her lips, joining him wholeheartedly in this dance.

*Cadeau is
French for gift.
Please accept
this invitation
to savor
the moment.
It is a gift.
Steal away
to adventure,
to laughter,
to love.
Leave behind
the frenzied rush of
a busy life.
Moments
stories are
alive and filled
with light-hearted humor
and captivating characters.
Each heartwarming tale
transports you to a place
where love and laughter
go hand in hand.
To a place where
the moments of love
last forever.*

MECHELLE AVEY

A LIFETIME LOVING YOU

A Cadeau Moments Book

This novel is a work of fiction. Names, characters, places and incidents are either the product of the author's imagination, or are used fictiously. Resemblance to actual persons, living or dead, events, or locales is entirely coincidental.

Published by
Cadeau Moments
a division of
Yeva Corporation
8362 Tamarack Village
Suite 119-PMB 284
St. Paul, Minnesota 55125

Copyright © 2001 by Felice Avey
Library of Congress Catalogue Card Number: 00-191135
ISBN: 1-930758-40-5
Visit our website at **http://yeva.com**

All rights reserved, which includes the right to reproduce this book or portions thereof in any form whatsoever except as provided by the U.S. Copyright Law. For information address Yeva Corporation.

First Cadeau Moments Paperback Printing: September 2000

Printed in the United States of America

If you purchased this book without a cover you should be aware that this book is stolen property. It was reported as "unsold and destroyed" to the publisher and neither the author nor the publisher has received any payment for this "stripped book."

To Regina Prather.
You are a true friend from God.
Inspirational. Invaluable. Irreplaceable.

Acknowledgements

My thanks to the people who worked so hard to make this book a reality. First, to Micaela Palumbo, you are a wonderful editor. Who knew one writer could make so many grammatical errors? Thanks to Hazel White, a future best-selling author, for being such a great help. Thanks Terry Gerritsen for not getting offended by idiotic comments, and for taking time out of your hot career to help mine. . . oh, and for letting me use your name in the book. I will always be a fan.

Thanks to my publicist, Pat Wafer, for reading my manuscript and for saying it was funny. Thank you for working so hard at promoting this book. Thanks as well to Becky Martin and Kurt Verlei for jump-starting the marketing machine. Kurt, I still say you're one of the best teachers I've ever had. Finally, thanks to my family. To Bryant and the munchkins, you guys are incredible, wonderful, talented, and patient. You've filled my life with blessings I can never repay.

By the way, Nance is named after Nan Martin, a very classy lady.

CHAPTER ONE

"Nance, you've got to help me!"

Cory Miller was drop dead gorgeous. A certifiable Adonis with squared jaw, smoke-blue eyes, and midnight-black hair. He reached across the high-gloss shine of a restaurant table and took Nance Hadley's hand.

His plea was made in a low, satin-smooth voice that brushed across Nance's flesh — an insubstantial promise which gave rise to an ache of longing inside her.

His eyes darkened, turning sapphire with the intensity of his appeal. "Please, Nancy-boo."

He was firing the big guns now, using his pet name for her.

Nance shivered and sighed, wishing for the hundredth time that she possessed some form of immunity against the entreaty in those thick-lashed eyes.

It was pathetic. Absolutely pathetic that she,

a woman of sound mind and a relatively high I.Q., could become a driveling, clueless idiot whenever Cory Miller asked her for something.

At least this time Cory had the cards deliberately stacked against her.

He'd done everything right, starting with an invitation to dinner at *Vignette,* the most romantic restaurant in the Twin Cities. The ambiance was intimate, with candlelight and muted classical music piped in against a backdrop of casual elegance. A fresh bouquet of roses was centered between them in a crystal vase. It scented the air, a seductive fragrance subtly hinting *l'amour.*

It was so right, and yet, so wrong, because *love* was the farthest thing from Cory's mind. At least, he wasn't thinking of Nance in those terms.

And that, really, was the problem.

"No way, Miller." Nance gently disengaged her hand from his. "I'm not a dating service."

"I know that." He dropped the suppliant pose. "But, you are my best friend. You're the only one I can ask."

Nance snorted. "You said you met this girl while you and Angie were out shopping, so ask Angie to help you."

Cory rolled his eyes heavenward. "Angie is a great sister. I love her dearly. But, I'd never have a chance if she got involved. The woman spends the bulk of her time talking to preschoolers. She thinks Barney the Dinosaur makes for fascinating conversation."

Nance's responding smile held no humor. She looked away, unable to hold his gaze. How could he ask her to help him? He knew how she felt about him. She toyed with her dessert fork feeling as though she'd been set up. "Let me get this straight. This whole *let me take you to dinner, Nance,* is your way of convincing me to play some kind of female Cyrano de Bergerac?"

"It's not like that." Cory's tone was defensive.

"Close enough."

"Don't make it such a big deal. I just want you to stop by the shoe store. Talk to Krystal Adkins. Tell her that she'd love working for us at Corance. Tell her she doesn't need to know anything about designing software."

"And?"

"And, if you can slip in a few compliments about me, then, even better." Cory's grin was beguiling. He should have had the grace to look embarrassed—his request was humiliating—but he didn't.

Nance rolled her eyes and took refuge in sarcasm. "I'm going to be sick."

"It's not like I'm asking you to write her a bunch of love letters," he pointed out. "I'm not trying to get you to feed me syrupy pickup lines. Just stop by the Foot Fetish."

Nance looked up at him, surprise freezing her features into comic amazement. "The Foot Fetish?"

Ignoring the incredulity of Nance's tone, Cory continued as though she hadn't spoken. "Stop by. Maybe you can convince Krystal to take the job. I'll handle the glowing testimonials for Cory Miller."

"I can't believe you're asking me to do something like this. It sounds like a really bad movie plot. Wait. That's exactly what it is, a bad movie: *The Seduction of Krystal Adkins*. News flash, Cor, the critics hate bad plots."

Cory was unmoved. He reached for her hand once more, his blue eyes imploring—*please, Nance*.

He removed the fork from her grasp. His ebony brows lifted in supplication.

Please.

He rotated her hand, facing it to him. Leaning toward her, his entire body focused into an unvoiced request, *Nance, please*.

His fingers slid over her palm, sending a tingling sensation along her arm, filling her body with a delightful warmth. In super slow-motion, he made feather-light circles across her skin, each rotation was an echo of one word: *Please. Please. Please.*

Her entire body quivered in response. She wanted him to continue but knew he would not. He was using her feelings against her, entreating her senses.

Frustrated, Nance pulled her hand away.

He was so beautiful.

His touch was so compelling.

It was so unfair.

She couldn't just give in. For her own self-respect, she had to fight. She tried another tack—direct confrontation. "This whole thing reeks, Miller. It's sleazy to the core."

"What's sleazy about offering the woman a job? Besides, I talked to her. She went to the same high school we did. We're just helping out an old school friend." Cory's voice was low and coaxing with a triumphant edge, as though he knew he'd won.

Nance forced herself to ignore her fluttering senses. It was his voice. It caused her to feel as if she were being wrapped in flowing silk. "Old school chum, or not, I've got two words, Miller—

sexual harassment."

Good. She sounded tough. Businesslike. She flashed him a hard, no-nonsense smile. He'd never know the quivering mass he'd made of her.

"The scenario, as I see it," she continued, "unfolds like this: Krystal Adkins takes your job offer. You do your song and dance number. She's not interested in the seduction part. What then, Cor?"

Cory sat back, his expression closed. When he spoke, his tone was so careful, Nance knew he was struggling to keep his temper in check. "What kind of a jerk do you think I am, Nance? If the answer is no, then, it's no—end of story. Krystal will have a good job—something better than part-time work in a shoe store."

He had it all worked out.

"Okay...." No-nonsense was failing her. She groped about for a new tactic and came up with logic. "Fine. You're Krystal's angel in disguise. You're not going to harass her, but she's already turned down the job. What could I possibly say that would make a difference?"

"I don't know. You're a woman."

With a statement like that, logic obviously had no place in Cory's mind.

"So . . . ." Irritation born of supreme frustration edged the word.

"So, talk to her," Cory urged, his tone filled with certainty, "girlfriend to girlfriend. Do the female bonding stuff."

"You sound like a sexist idiot."

"I don't know what they call this stuff."

"They call it ridiculous."

"C'mon, Nance. Nancy-boo."

"I'm not your Nancy-boo."

"I thought you liked that name."

"I haven't liked it since the second grade."

"Boo, then." Cory managed to sound injured. "Please, Boo. I would do the same for you."

"I wouldn't ask."

If Nance thought the coldness of her tone would change Cory's mind, she found herself sadly mistaken. Determination etched itself in the angled planes of Cory's face. "Nance, how long have we known each other?"

"I'm beginning to think too long."

"Don't get catty. It doesn't suit you."

"Maybe not, but . . . ." She stopped. *Don't say it*. The warning sounded inside her brain with the strength of a siren. *Don't tell him how you feel about him... again*.

It was good advice.

Nance knew she wouldn't take it.

It had been about three weeks since they'd last had what Nance now thought of as "*the talk*." They had "*the talk*" usually once every three-to-six months. This time the talk occurred after a day spent at the Minnesota State Fair.

The fair had become an annual event for Cory and Nance. They'd gone every year since high school. This year was no different. They'd spent a wonderful time eating everything in sight: roasted corn, pronto pups, chili fries, shaved ice, and funnel cakes. After the pickle-on-a-stick, Cory started feeling queasy.

Returning to Nance's home, Cory lay on the sofa and complained about how awful he felt, while Nance brewed herbal tea. Like a good little boy, Cory drank his tea. Then he laid his head in Nance's lap and fell asleep.

The sight of his handsome face, so vulnerable, so beautiful, caused Nance to let her guard down. Before she realized it, she was stroking his face, smoothing back the thick hair. Believing that Cory was sound asleep, Nance gave in to temptation. Leaning over, she placed a whisper-soft kiss on his lips.

The kiss woke him. For the briefest of moments, Nance thought Cory was kissing her back, but she grew flustered when he looked up at her with those devastating eyes.

She started babbling, the words tumbling one upon the other as she talked about how much she cared for him.

Abruptly, Cory sat up, robbing her of warmth. With a strained laugh he'd told her to stop imagining things, but he'd also added something new.

Maybe, he said.

Maybe someday, if neither of them found others.

Maybe.

He wasn't serious. She knew that. Over the years, he'd just found easier ways to let her down. At the time of the conversation, she'd been humiliated enough at the thought of being the last resort, that she'd sworn never to introduce the topic again.

It was a promise she was about to break.

She knew she was being foolish, but she had to try one more time to get Cory Miller to see what a great couple they would be: Cory and Nance, together forever.

"I think I have good reason to feel just a bit on the catty side."

There. The words were out.

In the reproach-filled silence that followed, Nance was left to wonder why she'd dared to think her words would change anything.

Cory's response was so painfully familiar.

How could she have forgotten the way he withdrew?

Physically. Emotionally. Spiritually.

Abruptly, he sat back, distant. His handsome features pulled into a frown. He refused to meet her stare, focusing instead on the bank of windows across from them.

Uncomfortable with the thought that he might shift his disapproving stare to her, Nance followed his gaze, and found herself wishing she hadn't.

Beyond the glass, the sky was velvet black, made almost starless by the brightness of a gigantic harvest moon. The entire scene was mirrored and softened, rendering nature into impressionism through the gliding wind that swept the surface of the massive lake beneath.

Lovers would enjoy the evocative beauty of the scene, would sense the subtle appeal to open, to join heart and mind and body.

Nance had spoken of joining, of opening up hearts to each other, but Cory was shutting her out. He was closing the door to her because she'd brought up her taboo feelings.

Bad Nance.

The silence continued, lasting overlong for

comfort.

Nance couldn't break the tension. She'd caused it. The humiliation that swamped her was so familiar. It was followed by shame. Sadness. Self-reproach. . . and relief. Relief that Cory had not yet spoken because silence, no matter how grim, was preferable to what she knew he would say.

"Not that again, Nance." The relief was short-lived. Cory spoke, his expression so full of disappointment that Nance felt like a drunk who'd fallen off the wagon.

"Sorry," she apologized, and felt pathetic.

She wanted to kick herself. She'd apologized for loving him. How utterly, utterly pathetic. "Cory, you're asking me to help you win another woman's affection." Was she whining? She hated whining. Her voice trembled, she knew that. Even she could hear the heavy emotion weighting the words.

Darn it, this wasn't how she wanted him to see her, but she couldn't seem to grab hold of any semblance of calm. How could Cory ask this of her? Couldn't he see that his request was akin to shooting daggers through her heart?

Couldn't he tell that she was holding onto sanity with slipping fingers; afraid that any moment now, she would fall on her knees and beg him to please not do this to her — to them?

Cory appeared genuinely surprised. "You can't possibly still think you're in love with me?" His tone was a mixture of amazement and irritation.

"I am in love with you. Still. I've loved you since the day we met."

"Yeah," Cory snorted. "And you gave me a conk on the head with a mud clod to prove it." He pointed to the almost invisible scar above his brow, offering a tepid smile, trying to introduce humor the way he always did when things got tense between them.

It was an easy out.

Cory was a master of the "humor technique," and now it was his gift to her, letting her save face.

To take it, she would have to deny her feelings.

Nance resisted him. "We were kids then," she said, twisting her cloth napkin into a circle around her index finger. "I haven't learned any better. God help me. I love you, Cory."

"Nance," Cory's satin voice was edged with a patience made annoying by its condescension. "I love you, too." He'd given her the speech often enough to have it memorized. "You're my friend, my best friend. You know I was joking when I said 'maybe.' You know that, right?"

"I know, Cory." How much more humiliation could she bear?

"Good. I couldn't stand to hurt you, Nancy-boo, because I do love you. I love you with all of my heart. I couldn't live without you . . . ."

"But — it's a different kind of love. . . ." Nance finished the sentence for him. Of course that was what he would say. He'd said it before. He'd said it over and over until she knew each painful word and even the inflection of his voice by heart.

Cory nodded, refusing to see anything in her recital but acceptance. "It's not the kind of love I feel for Krystal."

"Love?"

They'd been talking about that word, batting it about, giving little weight to it, but now, coming from Cory's lips in conjunction with another woman's name. . . Nance almost choked on it, sounding it out as though it were foreign, and she'd never heard it before. In a way she hadn't, at least not from Cory—not about a woman.

The only thing Cory loved, other than his 'friendship love' for Nance, was Sharla, his computer. "You love Krystal?" her voice sounded strangled. Self-consciously she cleared her throat.

Cory couldn't meet her eyes. "I'm sorry,

Nance. I feel like a real jerk."

The anger left her then. How could she blame him? He'd always been honest with her. She'd always known that this day might come. Succumbing to theatrics would only make a bad situation worse.

And, she still loved Cory. She couldn't bear to cause him pain.

"Don't," she said. Grimness laced her tone. She'd known forever that he didn't care for her the way she wanted. This whole scene was her own fault. She was the one who'd held on to the futile hope that "maybe" truly meant *maybe*.

She'd been a fool, grasping hope, believing that the platonic feelings Cory had for her could grow into something more.

He did care for her. It should be enough. Of course, it was cold comfort, but better that, than to be shut from his life completely.

Nance pasted a smile on her lips, ignoring the anguish that encased her heart in a frozen shell. "So, you love her?" The fragile smile held firm.

Cory couldn't hide his enthusiasm, not even for the sake of Nance's broken heart. "I do, Nance. I absolutely do."

"I'm happy for you," she told him. It was the ultimate lie, and speaking it fissured her heart to a state beyond repair.

Cory gave her an encouraging grin. "You're next," he said, telling his own lie, acting as though he really believed that someone would fall in love with her. "You'll find someone next."

Her fragile smile faltered. She let it die, wondering how she could breathe when the world about her seemed to be devoid of air.

She watched Cory as he chattered on about this girl, and she was returned to first grade. Cory Miller was the new boy in her class. From the moment she'd met him, he'd owned her heart.

Of course, first grade was a bit young to fall in love, but Nance had done so. She'd never changed her mind, not in the twenty-two years that she'd known Cory.

Over the years, they'd both dated, but the dates were so infrequent as to be nonexistent. In spite of his extraordinary good looks, Cory Miller wasn't a ladies man, had never been a ladies man.

His first love was computers. And Nance, with the precocious insight of an adolescent in love, had learned everything she possibly could about technology so that she could talk knowledgably on the subject with Cory.

Instead of *Teen Magazine*, she'd read *PC Magazine*, absorbing information on Macs,

Amigas, and personal computers.

Her reward for immersing herself in Cory's world had been that the two of them were inseparable. Nance, because she loved Cory enough to learn to love computers, and Cory, because Nance understood him.

They'd always been best friends. They were still friends, despite the difference in gender. And, they were friends despite the fact that Nance Hadley was as plain as Cory Miller was handsome.

Cory had stopped talking and now sat picking with desultory interest at the leftovers on his plate. Suddenly, Nance was taken with a burning curiosity. There was just one question, but it seemed the most important question of all.

"What does she look like?" Nance asked.

"Oh, Nance." Cory's voice actually shook with reverence.

Nance glanced sharply at him. The goofball. His eyes were glowing, focused on some invisible vision against which she could never compete.

"Krystal's like . . . like a fairy." His tone was one notch below worshipful.

Pain swept her, and the only weapon Nance had to defend against it was sarcasm. "Gee, a fairy, huh? Sounds just peachy."

"I'm serious, Nance." Cory met her gaze, his eyes blazing with passion. "She's like, five three, at the most. And, she's got tons of this wispy blonde hair. . . . Her eyes are huge. . . ."

"All the better to see you with."

Cory ignored her. "They're gray," he said, as if she hadn't spoken. "I swear, Nance. She looks like Tinker Bell."

"Tinker Bell, the cartoon, or Julia Roberts from Hook?"

"The cartoon."

"All these years I've known you, I never knew you had a thing for Tinker Bell."

"I have a thing for Julia Roberts, too." He motioned up and down with his brows, his Cory the lecher routine.

She'd seen it before. "Great." She smiled anyway. "I'd much rather hire Julia Roberts for our receptionist than someone described to me as a cartoon Tinker Bell."

"Then you'll do it?"

"I didn't say that." She should have known he'd see her participation in the light banter as surrender. Maybe it was. Sure, Cory was being deliberately obtuse, but Nance had no desire to keep fighting him. It was exhausting.

Besides, he had that look in his eye. The one

that said Cory Miller was going to get what he wanted—no matter what.

Tinker Bell didn't stand a chance.

Even Julia Roberts might have been tempted.

Cory was too attractive. He was too determined. Nance had never been able to resist him when he had that look. She doubted that Krystal Adkins would resist for too long.

"Cheryl doesn't even go on maternity leave for another month." It was all she had, a last ditch effort to resist the irresistible Cory Miller.

"Maybe not," no doubt he could see her resolve giving way, "but she'll need time to train someone."

Resolve? Had she ever possessed any when Cory was involved?

"Fine." Defeat weighted Nance's shoulders. Just fine. Cory would have his Tinker Bell.

What could she say about it anyway?

She had tried to prepare her heart, had tortured herself with various scenarios, but reality was far worse than she had ever anticipated.

She could do this, she reminded herself. She was strong enough to love Cory and to give him away to this Krystal person.

Regret flooded her. The pain of heartbreak had dulled to a familiar throb, but it was the regret that stung now. Regret that she'd never be beautiful enough for Cory Miller to love.

Like Cyrano de Bergerac, Nance Hadley was born plain.

Taken individually her features might have had a chance.

She had a fine, even smile. Her eyes were pale green, surrounded by thick lashes so blonde as to be invisible. Her mouth was full, maybe a shade too full, but it wasn't unpleasant. Her skin was peaches and cream clear.

They were features that should have been lovely together, but everything was thrust into confusion by her hair. Nance's hair was a throwback from some long dead Scot ancestor—probably a warrior. Had to be—for there was nothing that could tame the frazzled mane of hair. The color of a maple leaf in the fall, strands striated red and blonde and gold leapt outward into a massed bunch of wild, frizzed curls, full of electric energy.

Tonight she wore it pulled back into a puffy bun. Unconsciously, she smoothed an errant frizz back behind her ear. "So, what do you want me to do?" she asked Cory.

And that was that.

She'd said the words that set him free.

In spite of her agony, she couldn't help but feel his gladness as his lips stretched into an enormous smile.

She'd made him happy. And listening to him as he outlined what he wanted from her, her own pain receded a little.

Now she could feel that brief flutter of joy that came from loving someone unselfishly.

And Nance Hadley loved Cory Miller more than enough to ignore the shattering of her heart into a million fragments.

CHAPTER TWO

The entrance to the Foot Fetish was heralded by a gigantic, neon pink, stiletto-heeled pump with a matching pink paneled door located at the center of the arch.

Approximately fifteen minutes before closing time, Nance pulled her Aston Martin into a front row space at the strip mall where the store was located.

She felt conspicuous.

It wasn't the car. The silver DB7 was a convertible and sharp enough to compete with anything in the parking lot.

The problem was Nance. She sat in her *hotcha* car, staring up at the giant shoe, a frown of dismay marring the smoothness of her brow.

How had she allowed Cory to talk her into this?

Was love worth checking her brain cells at the

door while she blithely gave up the only man for which she'd ever cared—and that to a woman bearing a strong resemblance to a cartoon?

This was crazy, she decided. Instead of hanging out in the Foot Fetish parking lot, she should be making her way over to Health Partners for a visit to the psychiatric unit.

She'd have no trouble fitting in with the other rubber-room residents, but here at the Foot Fetish she was a trout in a puddle during fishing season.

As if to underscore the fact that she was seriously out of place, most of the shoppers she'd seen leaving with purchases were *bona fide* BARBS.

BARB was Nance's acronym for *Bubblehead Armed with Boobs*. Truth to tell, Nance had never seen so many BARBS in one place.

It was a convention of BARBS and—almost to an "*oh, baby*" one of them—the Foot Fetish BARBS wore updated weaponry in the form of stiletto heels.

Practical. That was the problem. Nance Hadley was far too practical to fit in with the Fetish demographic. Cory Miller, the Aston Martin, and an over-large lakeshore home were the only impractical things in her life; and many times she felt guilty for having indulged herself in those.

Nance sighed, wanting more than ever to forget the whole thing. After all, BARBS were dangerous women, James Bond sidekicks. They were the kind of women who eyed Nance and her frizzled, *notice-me* hair with looks of amused pity.

Love, nothing! She couldn't go in there. No matter how much she wanted to make Cory happy, she simply could not make herself get out of the car and go into the Foot Fetish.

A touch on her shoulder startled Nance out of her panic-stricken thoughts. She glanced up to find Cory. He grinned down at her, his smile a thousand watts bright.

"Lost in a world of dreams, are ya?"

"Cory!" She swatted at him and missed. "What are you doing here?"

"I figured you'd need moral support. After all, the Foot Fetish isn't really your kind of place."

"That's an understatement," Nance observed caustically. "What about you? Come here often?"

He shrugged, refusing to take the bait. "Just the one time with Angie. Haven't you ever been curious about this place?"

"No."

"Liar."

"Who could miss a giant, pink shoe?" she relented, but only a little. "Anyway, I can tell they don't sell loafers here."

"Is that the only type of shoe you own?"

"Loafers are practical." She sounded defensive.

"You should live a little, Nance. Throw out the sensible shoes. Buy some high heels. Do the town. Paint it as neon bright as the Fetish door. Conk some good-looking guy on the head and have yourself a shoe-gun wedding."

"As opposed to one instituted by a shot-gun?"

"Hey, a weapon's a weapon, and with stilettos, there's no waiting period."

"That's just funny enough to make me think about laughing. Out of pity, mind you."

Cory's answering grin was boyish and endearing. The sight of it caused Nance's breath to stop in her throat. Arms crossed over his chest, Cory leaned his rear against the side of Nance's car, his legs crossed at the ankles. He looked like an advertisement for male perfection.

The sight of him caused Nance's fingers to itch with the desire to wend a caress against the scratchy texture of his jaw, to draw him down to her, until their lips touched and breath mingled, and she could taste the sweetness of his kiss.

"Nance!" The insistent tone in Cory's voice suggested that he'd spoken her name more than once.

A LIFETIME LOVING YOU   31

"What?" Nance blinked and the pleasurable images dissipated against the fading sun.

"You've got five minutes before close. Are you going to do this or not?"

"What if I said 'or not'?"

"Then I'd have to tickle you." He wiggled his fingers menacingly.

"When are you going to grow up?" Nance asked, waving Cory back so that she could jump out of the car. She had little doubt that he would make good on his threat, embarrassing them both.

"Never!" Cory vowed, giving her a gentle poke in the side.

She slammed her door shut and introduced her elbow to his ribs. "All right, already. I'm going. You don't have to tell me twice."

"I was poking for the fun of it."

"You would. Are you coming with?"

"Nah, I'm going to hang out here, wait for you. We can grab a burger at Champps when you've accomplished your mission."

"Are you offering me a bone to make sure I don't back out? 'Do this, and you get a doggie treat?' I'm just asking because I need to know if I'm supposed to *woof* with joy."

"Forget the woof. Just go. Your bone will be waiting for you when you get back."

Cory strode ahead to pull open the door. Nearing the entrance, Nance slowed, but Cory was ready for her, and gave her a gentle push into the store. She glanced back at him, frowning severely at this treatment, but he just winked at her and let the door close in her face.

Nance sighed. The situation was worse than her worst nightmare. It was her worst nightmare times two. Not only was she giving away the love her life in the form of that selfish beast Cory Miller, she was giving him up to a BARB.

The thought rankled. That Krystal Adkins was a BARB, Nance had no doubt. She'd spotted Krystal immediately upon entering the store.

Cory was right. The girl did look quite a bit like a cartoon Tinker Bell. Only, Tinker Bell didn't have that tousled, ash-blonde hair cascading down her shoulders like a raging river.

Nor did Tinker Bell wear a red, midriff-bearing, vampire T-shirt sporting the words: "Love Bites" atop black, skin-tight jeans and black, three-inch spiked heels.

Yikes! Had Cory Miller lost his ever-loving mind?

Nance almost turned back then and there, but Cory, looking in through the window, motioned for her to go on.

Nance inched forward a couple of steps, feeling as if she'd fallen into a bad remake of Cyrano de Bergerac. Her best friend, the love of her life, her business partner, wanted to marry a former rock music groupie—in other words, a BARB *deluxe*.

Whatever. Nance could do this. She was the Cyrano.

And like Cyrano, she had no intention of letting anyone see how she really felt about the matter.

Taking a deep breath, she threw her shoulders back. Adopting an imitation BARB walk, she sauntered over to a stack of seriously sexy shoes, trying her best not to appear like a seriously dorky reject from the dog-ugly shoe club.

HOT! The words jumped out at her from a sign above a tiered stack of frosting-pink, clear-heeled stilettos. Nance eyed the shoes warily. She couldn't even begin to imagine squeezing her size-nine foot into a pair of those dainty hoofers.

"Not you," the voice came from behind her left shoulder.

Jumping as if she'd been caught stuffing the shoes into her handbag, Nance turned to find a man wearing a maroon jacket with an embroidered logo of a high heeled shoe over the name: Sugar

Smith, Manager.

"Those shoes aren't you," he said.

Speech-challenged, Nance stared. Sugar? The guy's name was SUGAR? The appellation seemed a gross mistake. Not only did Sugar not look sweet, he appeared the exact opposite of the word. Very obviously a body builder, Sugar topped off at around six feet with overdeveloped, muscular arms that bulged beneath a form-fitting gray T-shirt. His skin was a dark brown incongruously matched with hair that was bleached blonde and twisted into a disarray of short braids.

Sweet Stuff was a walking ad for jock central. Cool. Smooth. And, as her French aunt, Nan Martin, for whom she'd been named would say, "*tres bizarre.*"

Nance couldn't help but wonder what a ruggedly handsome, slightly scary-looking guy like that was doing working in a BARB shoe store.

Sweet and Low, or rather Sugar, grinned at her, and Nance noticed a small, gold hoop earring in his left ear. Used to computer geeks, code jocks, and conservative business professionals, Nance tried to remember what she'd heard about guys wearing an earring in the left ear.

Nothing.

She didn't have any frame of reference to fall

back on: this guy was truly out of her realm of experience.

"I beg your pardon?" Finally, she could speak!

His eyes were brown and brimming with amusement. "The shoes," he said.

Nance blinked. "Oh."

"I don't think I've seen you here before, have I?"

Was that a line? She remembered her looks and realized it couldn't be. No doubt, it was how they sold shoes at the Foot Fetish.

"No, this is my first time," Nance told him, her voice slightly husky from nervousness.

He smiled, his eyes crinkling at the sides, and she realized how provocative her answer sounded. He was polite enough not to point the double entendre out to her—Cory would have repeated it for weeks.

"I knew it," he told her instead. "I'm pretty sure I would have remembered a face like yours." He gestured at the wedding-cake stack of shoes. "Don't get me wrong, I think the shoes are nice, but they're not you."

"I couldn't agree with you more," Nance said firmly, wondering what he'd meant when he said that he would have remembered a face like hers. Surely they didn't have a policy against selling sexy shoes to dull-looking women?

Okay. Maybe she was being oversensitive. Not that it mattered. She wasn't at the Foot Fetish to buy shoes.

Nance turned from the shoes and caught a glimpse of Cory's face in the window. He was shaking his head and pointing at Tinker Bell. His message was clear.

"I'm not really here for shoes, anyway," Nance told the man, following Cory's cue. "I'm looking for Krystal Adkins."

Sugar gestured negligently behind him. "I just put her on the registers. She'll be finished in a few minutes."

Nance glanced in the direction he'd indicated and nodded. "Yeah. Thanks. I saw her when I came in. I'll just find an out-of-the-way spot and wait for her."

Sugar didn't seem to hear her. Almost as if he couldn't help himself, his eyes traveled in slow motion down to her feet. Nance resisted the urge to do a backward shuffle and hide her serviceable, low-heeled loafers.

When she'd purchased them the shoes had seemed so serious and businesslike, perfect for any use she might have for them. Now, however, they screamed *boring*.

And, of course, they were right. She was so boring that she didn't have anything better to do than to play matchmaker for the man she loved.

How amazing that shoes could be so revealing.

"You know," Sugar spoke in a slow, considering tone, "I've got the perfect shoes for you."

"You do?" It was not what Nance had expected him to say. After all, her shoes were shouting that she spent her Friday nights washing her hair and watching dull sitcom reruns on television— not dancing the night away in some trendy hot spot with the rest of the BARBS.

Surprisingly, she was curious about these perfect shoes; but no, she shouldn't even consider it. She was there for one purpose. The sooner she accomplished her goal and got out of Dodge, the better.

Besides, she had too much common sense to purchase a pair of shoes she'd never have an excuse to wear. She'd already seen what the Fetish had to offer. There wasn't a serviceable pair of loafers in the bunch.

"No," she repeated, more to herself than to Sugar. Regret laced her tone. "Thanks anyway... Mr. Smith." She pointed to his name tags and gave him her most charming brush off smile. "I'll just wait for Krystal. It wouldn't be fair to make you work when I have no intention of buying anything."

"I tell you what," Sugar countered. "Follow me. I'll find a seat for you. I'll also let Krystal know you're here."

"Thanks," Nance agreed gratefully.

"And, while you're waiting for her," he continued as though she hadn't spoken, "you can take a look at the shoes I've got for you."

"Well. . ." Nance glanced self-consciously back at the window. Cory was leaning against the giant heel. Thankfully, he wasn't looking inside. "I guess I could."

She had to wait for Krystal anyway. So, it wouldn't hurt to look, but she had no intention of being pressured into buying.

Her purpose there was painful enough. The last thing she wanted to do was to pay for the privilege of having her heart broken.

Sugar led the way through a number of different shoe displays, each and every one of them screaming: BARB BABE! He left her near the back of the store in a maroon chair with a silk-screened picture of a shoe on the seat.

Nance perched on the edge of the seat and looked around. Adjacent to the chair, there were several displays: one with jewelry, one marketing condoms—for conscientious BARBS, Nance supposed; and another with a tower of nail polish.

Clearly, the Foot Fetish was savvy in regard to cross-selling.

Nance glanced idly through the polish, but she could never imagine herself wearing colors like *Spicy Hot, Dangerous Rules, Dare to Bare*, or *Brash Babe*.

They were BARB colors.

"I've told Krystal that you're here." Sugar Smith had returned. Embarrassed to be caught studying the polish, Nance quickly pushed the bottle of *Peach and Passion* back onto the shelf.

She turned to find the most beautiful pair of shoes she'd ever seen, dangling from Sugar's upraised hand.

"Oh," she breathed, her heart tripping fast with excitement. "They're beautiful."

And they were.

Unlike most of the thin-strapped killer pumps the Fetish offered, these shoes were pure fantasy. There were two strips, one wide and one thin, of gold mesh that covered the top of the sole. The heel, made of a clear Lucite, was only an inch high instead of the requisite three- or four-inch height most BARBS favored. They were mules, though, with no back strap to hold them on.

Nance loved them.

"The reason these shoes are perfect for you is that they're classy and tasteful. They don't yell sex appeal, they hint it. We don't sell many of these shoes." Sugar handed the shoes into Nance's eager hands.

"Why not?" Nance couldn't imagine anyone not liking these beautiful shoes.

"They're called Night Dreams. They're a new product. The manufacturer's trying to position them for professional women, but we don't get a lot of profs in here."

"Really?" Nance pretended surprise, but she had the feeling Sugar wasn't fooled.

He shrugged. "These shoes are for women who don't need to advertise their femininity. They have skills other than, if you'll pardon the expression, bedroom bronc riding. These shoes are for three-dimensional women—smart, successful, and sexy—not our typical clientele."

"Oh." The excitement growing inside Nance died abruptly. As a partner in Corance Technology, she was successful. She was also smart—unless Cory was involved. But no one in his right mind would call Nance Hadley sexy.

She lightly fingered the gold mesh tabs. They

were so beautiful. She'd never wanted a pair of shoes the way she wanted these. *But they're sexy. You're not*, she told herself.

And where would she wear them?

"These shoes are you."

Nance's answer was accompanied by a bitter grimace. "Yeah, right."

"You don't believe me?"

"Look at me." Her tone was sharper than she meant it to be. "Uh, look, you don't have to talk me up. I know that I'm not sexy. I'm not beautiful. I'm not a BARB." Frustration with the whole scene took her over the edge. She placed the shoes on the floor and stood up. "I don't belong in here."

Sugar folded his arms and looked down at her from his superior height. "Who says?"

"Huh?" It wasn't what she'd expected him to say, and she didn't have an answer. Besides, why had she even begun this conversation? If this man couldn't see that she was plainer than dried mud, he must be blind—no, not blind. He just wanted to sell three-dimensional shoes to a two-dimensional woman.

"You are sexy," he told her. "Sexy is not about your shape. It's not about wearing so much makeup that you look like an advertisement for a paint store. Sexy is an attitude. Always. I try and tell that to my customers, especially the young girls who come in here wanting to attract a boy by dressing like *hootchies*."

"I beg your pardon?" Nance couldn't hide her smile.

"BARB, *HOOTCHIE*, it's interchangeable. You know the type. Insecure. Desperate. Trying to buy love by putting out."

"Oh." That wasn't Nance's definition of a BARB. She nodded anyway, like she'd met that type before. "A *hootchie*."

"A *hootchie*," he repeated, his eyes filled with amusement. He was laughing at her. He could tell that Nance wouldn't know a *hootchie* from a hole in the wall. "We get a lot of *hootchies* in here."

"You don't like *hootchies*?" Nance sat down once more. She was surprised that Sugar would hold such a view, considering that *hootchies*/BARBS made up a large part of his clientele.

Sugar shrugged. "I'm a man. Men love *hootchies*. They scratch a certain kind of itch, if you know what I mean. But when a man gets the itch to commit, then he's not looking for a *hootchie*." He stopped. "Well, not unless he's one of those old, moneyed buggers who takes a dose of *hootchie* to help him forget that he's heading out to pasture. Other than that, most men want somebody who has something going on up here." Sugar tapped lightly against his skull.

Nance was unconvinced. "And looks aren't important?"

"Sure they're important. I'd be a liar if I said different. Still, it's a total-package deal: not just looks, not just brains, not just doing something with her life."

"Interesting," Nance said. Actually, she found the conversation intriguing. In all the time that she'd known Cory, they'd never had a conversation about what men wanted from women. They'd never even talked about what Cory wanted from a woman. Nance had just watched and guessed, and modeled her behavior accordingly.

"So based on those criteria. . ."

"Based on those criteria, you're one of the sexiest women alive," Sugar finished for her.

Nance laughed. "You really want to sell these shoes, don't you?"

"I want to sell the shoes to you because they're a perfect fit, no pun intended." He bent down, picked up the shoes and offered them to her. She hesitated and then hefted them in her hand, weighing them like possibilities.

Shoes were just shoes.

They couldn't change a person's life.

Then again, her drab loafers shouted her story to the world.

Maybe she should follow Cory's advice. He'd told her to buy some frivolous shoes. "Conk some guy over the head with them," he'd said.

He was joking, of course.

Even so, the shoes tempted her with dreams of freedom from the loneliness that had engulfed her the moment Cory told her about Krystal.

Cory was in love with someone else. Despair flooded Nance. She closed her eyes, waiting for the sharp edges of pain to dull to a familiar throb. All too soon Nance would be shut out of his life. If she was truly serious about letting him go, maybe it was time she learned to live a little.

The shoes she held in her hand, the frivolous, BARB shoes, could be the first step in reclaiming her life.

Sugar put one foot up on the chair beside Nance and leaned forward. "I'm telling you the truth," he said. He laid his arm across his knee. Nance looked up from the shoes to find him staring at her. He was so close, she could reach out and touch his smooth, smooth face. From a distance, his eyes appeared dark brown, but close up, they were lighter, a caramel color. His expression was so intense, it set Nance to blushing.

"You are a very sexy woman," he repeated, his voice lowered to graveled baritone. He was beginning to convince her that he believed what he was saying.

Nance smiled, unsure of how to respond. Compliments like the ones Sugar Smith was handing out came few and far between in her life.

"Sugar!"

"Nance!"

She was saved by a loud duet of outrage.

Cory and Krystal were standing together behind Sugar. Neither appeared pleased.

Sugar pushed back from the chair. If he was embarrassed at being caught romancing a customer, he didn't give any indication of it. "You keep in mind what I said," he told Nance. He turned to Krystal. "Krystal, get Nance here a pair of Night Dreams in size nine narrow."

Krystal looked from Nance to Sugar and then back at Nance, a mutinous pout forming on her lips. "It's closing time," she said, folding her arms over her chest and glaring venomously at Nance.

"Not while we have customers." Sugar's tone left no room for argument.

"She's not a customer. You said she wanted to see me about something."

"She does."

Nance nodded vigorously. Embarrassment raised a red flush in her cheeks. Clearly, both Cory and Krystal must have heard the words Sugar spoke to her. Nance could only hope she was mistaken.

Krystal cast one last glare in Nance's direction and departed. Sugar went down on one knee before Nance, a knight in shining armor. He removed the shoe from her left foot. "I want you to trust me about these shoes." He looked up at her, giving her a quick wink.

Cory cleared his throat. "Before you start trying on shoes, could I have a quick word with you, Nance?"

"Sure." Nance gave Sugar an apologetic shrug.

"Alone," Cory added deliberately.

Sugar glanced from Nance to Cory. Standing up, he said, "I'll help Krystal find the shoes."

As soon as Sugar was out of hearing range, Cory turned to Nance and snapped, "Just what do you think you're doing?"

Nance was stung by his anger. "I'm doing what you wanted," she answered in a heated tone. He had no right to speak harshly to her. He'd sent her on this fool's errand of matching him up with the Queen of the Undead, and now he was practically yelling at her because she wasn't moving fast enough.

When would it end?

"No," Cory's assumed patience was patently artificial. "You're not doing what I wanted. You're buying shoes. You're flirting with an overgrown shoe salesman. What I wanted was for you to offer Krystal Adkins a job."

"I will," Nance explained, struggling to hold onto precarious equanimity. If this was how Cory behaved when he was in love, then maybe she was better off without him. Love was turning him into a real jerk. "I will," she repeated. "Krystal had to finish with the last of the customers, and I was waiting for her. Sugar told her that I was here."

Cory frowned. "Who's Sugar?"

"The manager." Nance glanced back and saw that Sugar was leaning against the counter beside the cash register. His eyes were on her. She wiggled her fingers in his direction. He responded with a wave. "Sugar," she said turning back to Cory. "The guy helping me."

"I don't believe this." Cory rolled his eyes skyward. "You're trying to pick up a guy named Sugar?" He drew her into a light embrace, gazing down at her with an expression of concern.

"Nance, the shoe-gun wedding thing was a joke."

It was the way he said it. His voice was full of amused affection. His tone fired the embers of Nance's anger. How dare he counsel her. How dare he talk in that condescending tone!

Nance pushed his hands away, breaking his hold on her. "Don't say another word," she hissed and skewered his chest with a manicured fingernail. Anger sliced through her like a hot knife. She ignored the hurt that followed it, and instead, fed the fury inside her.

No way was she taking Cory's cold comfort.

It was the anger that would carry her through and help her to survive her broken heart.

"Let's get a few things straight, Miller." She twisted her finger, punctuating the words with a jab to his heart. "First, I'm not trying to pick up anyone, least of all Sugar. Second, you're way out of line, buddy. I'm here to help you out. If I want to dance the hula doe-naked on top of the biggest shoe display in the store, there's nothing you can say about it. Are we clear?"

It was the first time Nance Hadley had ever caused a scene amid a stack of stilettos. It felt good. A sense of power filled her. She jabbed Cory's chest one more time for emphasis.

"Oh, I'm clear alright," Cory spat the words

at her. "You're the one who's confused."

"I'm confused?" she repeated, her eyes wide with challenge.

"You're confused."

Nance crossed her arms. "Clear it up for me then."

"I asked for your help because I thought I could trust you."

Oh, yeah. She'd forgotten that logic wasn't Cory Miller's strong suit. "I'm here, aren't I? Fool that I am."

"You're here, but instead of doing what I asked, you're making goo-goo eyes at a man who wears earrings."

Logic flew from Nance on blazing wings of anger. *"Goo-goo eyes?"* Her expression showed her derision. "You've got to be kidding. Who writes your material, one of Angie's kids? I wasn't making *goo-goo* eyes at anyone. For your information, Sugar might wear an earring, but at least he has the courage to speak his mind and not let someone else do his dirty work for him."

Cory's reply was interrupted by Sugar, who called from across the room, "Nance, we've got your shoes. You want to try them on, or just ring them up?"

"Ring them up, please," Nance answered, her

eyes trained on Cory in a heated glare. "Look, if you don't like my methods, fine. Fire me and do your own dirty work. Otherwise, stay out of my way because you already owe me, Miller." She flicked back a strand of frizzy hair. "And you owe me big."

"Why are you being so hostile, Nance?"

Now he was accusing her of being hostile? Nance ground her teeth together to prevent herself from screeching invective. Striving mightily for that seemingly unattainable calm, she said, "I agreed to do this because of my feelings for you. I didn't agree to be hounded and critiqued every step of the way."

"I'll stay out of your way then." Cory stepped back, but added nastily, "Quit wasting time."

Nance didn't bother to reply. She lifted a disdaining eyebrow at Cory and then turned in a huff, stomping away in an up, down, up, down march. It wasn't the least bit dignified, because Sugar still had her other shoe, but she didn't care. She only wanted to put as much distance as possible between herself and Cory.

How could she have fallen in love with such a numbskull? It was a question she couldn't answer. She only knew that she had loved him. She did love him. Even now, every time she looked at

A LIFETIME LOVING YOU 51

Cory, her heart threatened to stop beating.

It wasn't fair.

Somehow, she would find a way to stop her heart from yearning for Cory Miller.

Krystal came from the storeroom. Joining Sugar at the register, she watched in derision as Nance made her way up to the counter.

Nance caught the disdain in the girl's gaze and issued a harassed sigh.

Now what? She wondered. Why was Krystal's behavior so antagonistic? Ignoring the girl's scornful expression, Nance plastered her most professional smile on her lips.

"I'm Nance Hadley." She extended her hand.

Krystal ignored it, until Sugar, unobtrusively, elbowed her in the ribs. Briefly, she gave Nance the tips of her fingers.

Nonplussed, Nance released Krystal's fingertips and turned to Sugar, who handed over her other shoe. In one quick motion she bent and slipped the loafer onto her foot.

Both feet shod, she faced Krystal once more.

"We went to school together. I guess you were two years behind Cory and me."

She doubted that the girl would recall her from as far back as high school, after all, it was a little over ten years ago, but at this point, Nance didn't care whether Krystal could remember her or not.

She was sick to death of this whole stupid scheme. She wanted nothing so much as to offer Krystal the receptionist job at Corance. After that, she would go home and nurse her broken heart in blessed isolation.

"Oh, yeah," Krystal's tone was sour. "You're that girl they used to call *Frizzy Tizzy*."

Nance felt her heart sink. Krystal did remember. Worse than that, she was rude enough to remind Nance of the cruel name she'd been called by some of the kids in school.

Wonderingly, Nance glanced back at Cory. This was the woman of his dreams?

She was obnoxious.

What in the world could he possibly see in her?

What did this awful girl have that Nance didn't?

Looks. Returning her gaze to Krystal, Nance found the answer to her question. For a moment the girl's odious behavior had served to blind her to Krystal's delicate beauty.

Unfortunately, Krystal's beauty was only an inch deep. The rest of her, her manner of dress, her attitude, her behavior, were unprofessional, antagonistic, and sarcastic. . . and, in Nance's opinion, that was just a start. She ignored the thought that her assessment of Krystal might be born of sour grapes.

After all, it was clear that Krystal's negative attitude was habitual. Nance had barely spoken ten words to the girl. There'd been no time to earn Krystal's dislike.

"Yeah, high school kids, huh?" Nance's smile was short enough, although she played along, pretending that the girl's discourtesy was humor.

Krystal shrugged. "You haven't changed much." She held up the Night Dreams. "So, are you going to buy these shoes?"

"I suppose I am." Nance spared another glance back at Cory. He'd finally gotten over his snit. He grinned self-consciously and gave her a thumbs up signal. There was no two ways about it, Cory Miller was a jerk. Nance was well rid of him.

"You want me to tell your boyfriend that you're almost done?" Sugar had noticed the exchange.

Nance shook her head, but directed her response to Krystal. "Oh, he's not my boyfriend," she explained in a loud voice. "He's my business partner."

Krystal slanted an arch glance in Sugar's direction. "He's the one I told you about. The rich guy. He asked me out."

"Lucky you." Sugar's lack of interest was obvious enough to be insulting.

Krystal clenched her teeth. "Yeah," she agreed grimly. "Lucky me. He also offered me a job. In fact, he offered about twenty grand more than I make here."

"Really?" Sugar looked from Nance to Cory. "He's a business partner, not a boyfriend?"

Nance nodded, and felt compelled to add, "And a friend." Although, at this point, Cory's status as a friend was under serious review.

Sugar was dubious. "He seemed awfully upset about the compliment I gave you. I thought he was a jealous boyfriend."

A sudden, sharp pain paralyzed Nance into immobility, and then it subsided, easing into the familiar dull throb that now seemed a permanent lodger in her chest. "Nope." She swallowed around a lump of distaste and forced herself to continue. "He is interested, however, in having Krystal come and work with us at Corance."

It wasn't how she'd planned to present Cory's case, but nothing was going the way she'd hoped. Krystal and Sugar were both so unconventional. Nance figured it was time to lay her cards on the table. She'd come to the Foot Fetish to offer

Krystal a job, not to be ridiculed, and not to buy shoes.

"That's why I'm here actually," she told them.

"Oh?" Krystal drew the word out. She slanted a gaze at Sugar and then looked past Nance to Cory. "*He* sent you to offer me a job?"

Nance wasn't sure she liked the implication that she was nothing more than Cory's errand girl, but then, in this instance, it was true. The lump in her throat was back. Nance swallowed and nodded in agreement.

Immediately, Krystal's face transformed, her animosity disappearing like sleight of the hand magic.

She ran the Night Dreams over the scanner. "I see," she said, suddenly as perky as a cat with cream. She hit the total button on the register. "Sixty-five dollars even." Her tone was cheerful.

Sixty-five dollars for a pair of shoes that were barely there? Nance pulled her wallet from her purse and rummaged through it, looking for her check card. She finally located it and handed it to Krystal, reflecting that what she was really paying for was being a fool. Of course, if she looked on the bright side of the situation, at least now she had shoes to wear to Cory's wedding.

"Is your husband a part of this partnership?"

Sugar asked casually as he put Nance's purchase in a sack.

"Oh, I'm not married," Nance answered him before turning back to Krystal. "Please, Krystal, give the offer some thought." She glanced at Sugar. "And, Mr. Smith, I hope you will forgive me for trying to steal your employee."

It really was bad form to solicit Krystal directly in front of her manager, but Nance felt that she had no choice. Cory's presence behind her spured her on to accomplish the task. The last thing she wanted was for him to make anymore unfounded accusations about her and Sugar.

Sugar waved off Nance's apology. "Krystal should take the job. I've told her repeatedly that she's wasting her time around here."

The words seemed to anger Krystal. She drew herself up into an indignant huff. "You know why I stay," she said stiffly.

"And you're wasting your time."

"I don't think so."

"I do," Sugar's response was certain. His expression was carved from stone.

"Is that your last word on the matter?" All at once, Krystal seemed weary. Watching her, Nance wondered what about the exchange had caused her to lose her cheeky attitude.

"That's the word," Sugar said. He looked over at Nance. "So, Nance, you're not married, and Krystal's knight doesn't belong to you. Tell me you're not seeing anybody, because I'd like to get your phone number."

Nance blinked. "My what?" she asked, so stunned she almost fell over backwards.

"Maybe we could go out for dinner?"

A date? The manager of the Foot Fetish, whom she'd just met, was asking her out on a date? Nance stared uncomprehendingly at Sugar, aware that some type of response was called for, but feeling completely incapable of making one.

And then, at last, a flaring of insight, it finally dawned on Nance that the reason Krystal Adkins worked at the Foot Fetish was not because she was a BARB who lived for shoes. She was in love with Sugar Smith.

The revelation filled Nance with wild relief.

If Krystal was in love with Sugar, then Cory was safe. At that moment, Nance wanted nothing more than to throw her arms around Sugar's neck and plant a blubbering, slobbery kiss of thanks on his lips.

Before she had the chance to disgrace herself, Krystal spoke up. "I think I'll take you up on that job offer, Frizzy." Krystal handed Nance her shoes in a pink-neon bag. Gaze chilly, she told Sugar, "Consider this my resignation. After all, there's absolutely no reason for me to hang around here."

Nance's feelings of relief died an agonizing death. "Great," she replied, but now that she'd accomplished her goal, she found herself unable to continue. It was as if the world had come crashing down on her, a mountainous pile of blackness that blinded her completely.

At the back of her mind, Nance had kept out the hope that Krystal would refuse the job. She'd already turned the offer down once before and her attraction to Sugar gave her ample reason to want to keep her current job.

Moreover, Nance didn't really want Krystal at Corance.

It was one thing to know that Cory was pursuing another woman—an unsuitable one at that—it was quite another thing, however, to be forced to watch the chase.

"Great," Nance repeated her frozen loop recording. Krystal was going to take the job. Somewhere, lost in the fog of her awareness, Nance knew that this was the time to talk about next steps: when Krystal could start, what she could expect in terms of training, the name of the person to contact upon her arrival at work.

Instead, Nance gaped helplessly in Cory's direction.

Krystal took matters into her own hands. "Cory," she yelled, motioning for him to join them at the counter. "Old Frizzy here has me convinced that you're the man, and Corance is the plan." She put a hand on her hip, jutting it out in a provocative manner. With an obvious sideways glance at Sugar, she drawled, "So, handsome, I'm ready to sign on the dotted line. When do I start?"

Cory rubbed his hands together, eyeing Krystal as though she were a thick, chophouse steak. Watching him, Nance thought either she would be sick, or she would smack Cory a good one for putting her through this.

Did the man have no sensitivity?

Of course he didn't. The next words out of Cory's mouth made that point heartbreakingly clear. "That's something we need to discuss as soon as possible," he said, flashing Krystal his most charming smile. "Do you have any plans after work?"

Krystal slanted another sideways glance in Sugar's direction. "Nope."

"Good! That's just great." Cory sounded like an overeager teenager. His hearty good humor was definitely beginning to irritate Nance. His gaze encompassed both women as he said "Why don't we make this informal? We can go out, have fun, a company-get-together-employee-orientation kind of thing."

"Love to, don't'cha know." Krystal rolled her eyes, but Cory was oblivious.

"Good. How about bowling?"

Bowling? Nance stared at Cory in shock. Cory Miller hated bowling. He was more of a walk-in-the-park, let's go to the symphony type. Yet, in typical Cory fashion, he'd done his homework. Cory was meticulous to a fault. It was that quality that made him a great programmer. It was that quality that made him a great business partner. But it hurt, darn it, to see Cory using that diligence on behalf of this overblown Tinker Bell.

It was proof that Cory Miller had fallen in love at last.

He obviously knew what Krystal liked. He was ready to transform himself into the man Krystal wanted.

Just like Nance had transformed for him.

Some perverseness of nature induced Nance to ask, "What about the burger you promised me?"

"Bowling alleys have great food," Cory observed.

"He's right," Krystal joined in, finally showing a glimmer of animation—over bowling, no less.

Nance hefted her shoe bag more firmly in her hand. "You guys have fun," she said. Before she could make her escape, however, Cory caught her arm, holding her in a firm grasp. "You're coming, too, Nance."

As a tag-along? Nance was surprised that he even wanted her there, but she'd endured enough humiliation for one night. "Thanks, but no." She shook her head. "You know I don't bowl. Besides, three's a crowd. You can go over the particulars without me."

"I don't bowl either, Nance. I'm going to need your help." Cory's gaze was imploring.

He really did want her along. Why, Nance had no idea, unless he wanted her to take up the slack if conversation faltered. She could talk him up to Krystal. She could introduce Cory's name as powder room conversation. There were a number of things she could do to help Cory win Krystal's affection, but enough was more than enough.

Nance was no knight in armor. She couldn't keep running to the rescue every time Cory wanted something. Beyond that, she had her own heartbreak to deal with.

All of these years she'd waited and longed and hoped. And now, she'd lost. Cory was riding off into the sunset with someone else. Nance couldn't keep pretending that it didn't hurt. She couldn't keep playing this game, not without a break.

She'd done what Cory had asked of her. She'd helped him connect with Krystal.

Now, it was time for her to step back—let go.

"No, Cory." The words were forced from the deepest part of her. Nance couldn't think of a time that she'd ever, before, said 'no' to him.

Cory's expression was surprised. "No?"

"No." Nance was definite, her tone deliberate. "I'm not going with you."

"I think I have a solution." Sugar had been watching them, watching Nance.

"What?" Cory's eyes flicked over Sugar's blonde twisted braids and his muscle-bound physique with derision.

Sugar ignored his condescension. Coming from behind the counter, he surprised them all by taking one of Nance's hands into his own. He raised her hand to his lips, brushing a feather light kiss across it. Nance blushed a fiery red, but couldn't staunch the feeling of triumph at having Cory see that another man found her attractive.

"You don't subject a lovely woman like this

to running behind you like a third wheel," Sugar said, addressing Cory. "Why don't I come along, even things up?"

Nance couldn't help but feel surprised at his thoughtfulness. Sugar was still giving her compliments, even though she'd already bought the shoes. Perhaps she'd stumbled onto their customer loyalty program.

"Oh, no, Sugar," she told him, charmed in spite of her doubts, "You don't have to do that. Although it's very kind of you." Nance waved her hands in front of her, her bag bumping against her knees.

"I think it's a great idea," Krystal put in enthusiastically. "Bowling with two people isn't that much fun anyway."

Cory didn't appear overly thrilled about including Sugar, but it was a ready solution to his dilemma. "Sounds good to me." He shrugged. "Nance? I didn't mean to make you feel like a third wheel. C'mon, come with us."

Nance shook her head, adamant. "I can't." She inched backward, moving in what she hoped was the general direction of the door. "I've got a lot going on tonight."

"Oh, let her go," Krystal said pettishly. "We don't really need Frizella anyway, do we guys?"

Krystal looked from Sugar to Cory and then back to Sugar. "The three of us can do individual bowling."

Cory grunted noncommittally, but Sugar directed a stern glance in Krystal's direction, saying, "There's nothing less attractive than a woman who calls someone else names, or makes fun of something that can't be changed. I think Nance has beautiful hair."

"You do?" A trio of voices queried.

"I do." Sugar turned his warm gaze on Nance.

"Thank you," Nance was touched by his kindness. The thought struck her that Cory, the man she'd loved since grade school, had done nothing, had said nothing to defend her.

Sugar Smith, on the other hand, had acted the part of a gentleman from the moment she'd met him, in spite of his bleached braids, in spite of the funky earring in his ear.

Suddenly, Cory Miller's blue eyes didn't seem so appealing.

Sugar lifted his shoulders in a deprecating shrug. "I'm just telling the truth."

"Nance," he said, his brown eyes sincere, "I'd like to get to know you better, and I think tonight would be a great time to start."

God help her, there was genuine interest in

those eyes. Beyond that, he'd shown her true kindness. It was so much more than she'd ever gotten from Cory.

The frozen shroud around Nance's heart seemed to thaw a little. And, for the first time in her life, Nance didn't care what Cory wanted her to do. She would go with them—because of Sugar.

She felt an alien stirring of interest. Maybe she wanted to get to know him better too.

Ignoring the hostility in Krystal's expression, and disregarding the startled dismay on Cory's face, Nance reached out and placed her hand on Sugar's arm.

"Yes," she told him, loving the light that flared in his brown eyes as she spoke the word. "I'd love to go bowling with you."

CHAPTER THREE

"Good grief, Nance, you're acting like a desperate old maid!"

Temper cinched to a hair's breadth of breaking free, Nance kept her eyes trained on the road, but even the forced concentration didn't keep her from burning hotter than a camp fire gone astray as Cory ranted and raved from the passenger side of her car.

They were on their way to Retro Bowl in Maplewood where, within the hour, they were scheduled to meet Krystal and Sugar. Krystal had gone home to change clothes, while Sugar would join them after closing out the day's receipts.

A change of clothes appealed to Nance too, but Cory had insisted on climbing into her car and reading her a non-stop riot act.

"I don't know what's going on in your mind," he told her as they pulled out of the Fetish parking lot, "but I'm concerned."

"What could you possibly have to be concerned about?" A headache had formed at the base of Nance's skull. It moved forward now, a throbbing, painful reminder of her heartbreak.

"What could I be concerned about?" Cory's stare was incredulous.

"Is there an echo in here?" Nance flashed Cory a brief grin, hoping the bit of levity would help.

It didn't.

The frown between Cory's brows deepened. "So now you're a comedienne?" He didn't wait for a response. "Nance. Do you realize what you've just done?"

"Made a bad joke?" She tried humor again, but instead of relenting, as he usually did when Nance teased him, Cory closed his eyes. He appeared to be counting to ten. "Nance, I'm trying to have a serious conversation." He opened his eyes and pinned her with a direct stare. "Maybe you could join me?"

Cheerfulness evaporating, Nance slanted a cautious glance sideways at Cory before returning her eyes to the road. "You want serious? Fine. I haven't the faintest clue what you've got to be upset about. " Nance's fingers gripped the steering wheel tightly, the only sign of her agitation as she spoke in a clear, even tone. "I've done everything you've asked of me, Cory. From my perspective, you should be on the ground kissing my feet, not yelling about how concerned you are."

Cory snorted. "This isn't about me." He shook his head, an expression of sincere wonder on his face. "You don't get it, Nance, do you?"

"What's to get?" Nance returned. She was tired of placating. If he wanted a fight, then he'd get a good one.

Cory rifled a hand through his thick hair and sighed. When he spoke again, his tone was gentle, disarming her with warmth. "Look, Nance, I know that you're feeling a little mixed up right now. Maybe you want to get back at me for this Krystal thing, but that's no reason for you to go around picking up complete strangers."

"Get back at you?" A buzzing sound filled Nance's ears, a rush of blood that pounded through her—the dam of anger released. She opened her mouth to say the words that would blast Cory's arrogant assumptions into a million pieces, but found that she was speechless. Like a fish caught on a hook, her mouth formed into a frozen 'oh.'

She waited for the connection to resume between mind and speech. A sour anger coated her tongue so thick, she doubted her ability to move it enough for dialogue.

Finally, struggling to keep her voice calm after a tension-filled silence that seemed to have lasted an eternity, she said, "I take it you're talking about Sugar Smith?"

"Unless you've been trolling for strangers elsewhere. Yeah, I'm talking about Sugar Smith. Cripes, Nance, you don't even know the guy, and you're drooling over him like a pimply faced teenager."

At that, Nance almost hit the brakes. One abrupt pump on the pedal would send Cory and his goof-ball accusations flying through the air. But no. Firing Cory out of the car into the current of I-94 traffic would only make a bad problem worse.

She sighed. What in the world had gotten into Cory Miller anyway? Never, not in all their twenty-plus years of friendship, had he ever treated her with anything but an affable, good-natured friendliness. Sure, they'd had an occasional tiff. After all, they were in each other's pockets almost continually. But, for the most part, they got on splendidly.

This new Cory Miller—with his selfish demand that she help him connect with Krystal, and his almost-jealous comments regarding Sugar Smith—was disturbing.

"Sugar's not a stranger." Nance chose her words with care. "He works at the Foot Fetish. He's the manager, for crying out loud. What more does the man need to recommend him? I know people who've gotten married on less than that."

"See!" Cory was practically shouting. "See what I mean!"

"No, I don't," Nance struggled to maintain her calm. Nothing would be gained by getting upset, but even so, she was beginning to feel that patience as a virtue was overrated.

"You've known the man how long? Fifteen minutes? Twenty minutes, tops, and yet, you're talking about marriage."

"I am not talking about marriage. It was just an example."

"An example of what?"

Nance turned her eyes from the congested traffic to glance briefly at Cory, a puzzled expression on her face. Maybe this thing with Krystal was causing him to overheat. Perhaps he'd fried a circuit board in his brain or seared a synapse while waiting for Nance to tell Krystal about his offer.

"Forget it, Cory." Nance shrugged. "You're completely overreacting."

"I don't think so," he told her, although he did moderate his tone. He faced her in the car.

"Nance, I'm your best friend. There's no way I'm going to stand by and watch you make a huge mistake just because you're rebounding."

The comment stung. No. It infuriated.

"What do you mean I'm rebounding?"

"You know what I mean," Cory said the words without one hint of self-consciousness.

"From you?" Heart-sore, Nance took refuge in sarcasm.

At last, Cory had the grace to look embarrassed. "You said you were still in love with me."

"I did, didn't I?" Abruptly, Nance swerved into the parking lot of the bowling alley and swung the Aston Martin into the nearest parking space. Switching off the ignition, she sat with hands draped lightly atop the steering wheel.

She couldn't look at Cory.

He was the man who'd rejected her.

He'd broken her heart.

She wasn't certain if she'd ever recover, but she did know that the worst thing she could do was to sit at home moping about the changes taking place in their relationship. Cory was moving on with his life. Nance had to do the same.

Hands moving down to grip the steering wheel with inflexible fingers, she said, "I told you I loved you. I asked you for the chance to make you happy. We both know your answer." She smiled a little, to take the sting from her words. "No, I'm not rebounding. I'm letting go. No more begging. No more pleading. You're free."

Cory listened to her, almost as though he were hearing her for the first time. He was so still that he appeared carved from marble.

"You're free," Nance repeated.

For a moment, she thought she saw a hint of sadness in Cory's eyes, but if so, the expression was brief. He sighed and ran his fingers through his dark hair, sending it into disarray. Watching him, Nance was struck again by his good looks but, he was not for her. He wanted Tinker Bell. He wanted something Nance could never be.

Her thoughts strayed to Sugar Smith. Sugar thought her hair was pretty. She smiled remembering how the comment had stunned them all. It gave her the courage to meet Cory's reluctant gaze with a defiant glare. "Besides, I like Sugar."

It was the straw Cory needed. "He's the manager of a shoe store, Nance. You're a partner in a firm valued at thirty-five million dollars."

"On paper," she pointed out.

"You take home half a million a year in salary. You own stock valued at seven million."

"Even so, I didn't like spending sixty-five dollars for a pair of shoes so that you could get a date with a shoe-store clerk."

"Just because you're cheap doesn't mean that you're not an easy mark."

"You think Sugar marked me?"

"Yes."

She pretended to consider the idea. "You're right," she said after a moment. The flat of her hand pressed against her forehead. "I remember now. Sugar was scanning the stock market page when I walked into the Foot Fetish. And knock me over with a two-ton feather if he didn't take one look at me and say, 'Here comes my sugar mama. She's got enough stock options to keep me in high-heeled shoes for the rest of my life.'"

"Don't be ridiculous." Cory couldn't hide the twitching of his lips.

"Who's being ridiculous? That's how it happened, at least, in your mind."

All the humor drained from Cory's face. "I'm just trying to make you see reason. I don't want you to get hurt."

He didn't want her to get hurt? What could she say to that, when he was the one who'd broken her heart?

"Too late," she choked. Why couldn't he just let it go?

Cory glanced sharply at her. "What do you mean, too late?"

"You've already broken my heart, Miller." The tears she'd held back all evening finally spilled in a rush onto her cheeks.

"Oh, Nance." The fight left Cory. Awkward with compassion, he took her into his arms, holding her tenderly, the way she'd always dreamed he would.

For a moment, she allowed herself to pretend. She pretended that Cory returned her love, that he wanted her as much as she wanted him. Nestled in his arms, the dream was easy to believe. His warmth enveloped her. His arms were strong around her.

At once, the love that she wished dead and buried, bloomed like a rose against the chilled barren space of her heart.

"I'm so sorry, Nance," Cory's words were delivered in a hushed voice, his warm breath stirred the curly wisps of her bangs.

Tears drying, Nance looked up at him. It was clear that this time, his apology was more than the response of guilt. He finally seemed to understand just how much she cared.

"I wouldn't have fallen in love with Krystal if...."

"If what?" Nance interrupted him. "Don't lie, Cory. Don't make this worse by making things up."

"I don't want to hurt you, Nance."

Somehow Nance found the strength to lift her head from Cory's arm, to walk away from pretense. She eyed him with a resoluteness that she'd never realized she possessed. "I will survive," she said, and meant it. "Don't waste your time feeling guilty."

"I can't help it." He lifted her chin, his thumb gliding over her cheek, light strokes that soothed her. His eyes dropped to her parted lips. He swallowed. The sound was loud in the air between them. "I don't want to cause you pain, Nance. I want you to be happy."

Nance watched, spellbound, as he brought his face close to hers, and then his lips brushed across her own in a fleeting kiss of incredible sweetness.

"You're not being fair," Nance whispered. Involuntarily, her eyes closed. She wanted him to kiss her again, even the brief kiss of a friend.

Of course, he didn't.

He wouldn't.

Nance opened her eyes to find his gaze still on her lips. Self-consciously, deliberately, he moved back. "I know."

Nance sighed, seeing the movement as rejection of the love she offered him. "Then let me make my own decisions. I've done that for you. I'm letting go. You have to let go, too."

"Let go of what?"

Nance turned from him. "Of me. If Tinker Bell is who you want, then you have to let go of me. Don't expect me to play chaperone. I'm not going to tag along anymore, like a third wheel, so things are easier for you. Don't call me when there's a problem. Don't use me."

"Use you?" Cory snorted. "Where is this stuff coming from? How can you think that I use you?"

Nance's smile was a bitter twisting of her lips. "Nance, please," she parroted in a perfect imitation of Cory's tone, if not the timbre of his voice. "Please, you've got to help me."

Cory crossed his arms over his chest. "Friends help each other. That's not using you."

"Then help me, Cory," Nance said. "Help me have a great time with Sugar. Don't judge. Don't preach."

"Don't care. Is that what you want, Nance?"

"If that's what it takes for both of us to let go, then yes. How do you think I'm bearing all of this. I keep telling myself I don't care."

"You care."

It was a truth from which she couldn't hide. "I care. Yeah. I care, but, I'm moving on."

"Does that mean we're no longer friends?" Cory's tone was wooden.

Nance swung to face him, her hand finding his. "No," she exclaimed. "Oh, no, Cory. It doesn't matter who you marry. It doesn't even matter if we never see each other, or even speak to each other except at the office. I will always be your friend."

"I'll always be yours, Nance."

"I hope so. Because sometimes love separates friends."

"Then can I say one final thing, as a friend."

Nance sighed, realizing that he'd outmaneuvered her. "What?"

"Be careful."

"I think you've got more to worry about than I do. After all, Tinker Bell likes to sharpen her claws on a regular basis."

"What's that supposed to mean?"

"You don't know?" Nance still couldn't believe that Cory would countenance Krystal's insulting behavior, but, thus far, he'd made no mention of it, preferring to concentrate on Nance's innocent overtures of friendship with Sugar Smith.

Cory's uneasy gaze faltered before Nance's

emphatic stare. His wasn't the sin of oblivion. He knew Krystal's behavior was beyond the bounds of propriety, and it hadn't mattered enough for him to speak out.

The realization swept over Nance, shredding tender feelings with a sharp knife.

"I'm sorry about the way Krystal behaved," Cory spoke after a moment. "I don't know why she was being so unfriendly."

Nance shrugged. If Cory couldn't see that Krystal was in love with Sugar Smith, then she wasn't about to clue him in. Besides, Nance had little doubt that Cory's charm would eventually win him what he wanted.

At the moment, everything was muddled together. Cory preferred Krystal, who wanted Sugar, who seemed interested in Nance, who foolishly carried an ancient torch for Cory.

It was worse than a soap opera.

And in true soap-opera fashion, Cory was the only one who didn't know Krystal's real feelings. Nance resisted the urge to prick Cory's arrogance by informing him of the reason behind his beloved's resistance to his overtures. Yet, no matter how angry and hurt she felt by his rejection, she had no intention of being the destroyer of his dreams.

Suddenly, Cory sat up. "There's Krystal!" he said, snapping Nance from her dismal thoughts. He pointed to a shapely figure making her way through the parking lot.

Nance couldn't help but stare. Krystal still wore the skin-tight, black jeans, but she'd replaced the Vampire tee-shirt with a cream colored, midriff-bearing, bead sweater. Even more dramatic was the change to her hair. As Krystal drew closer, Nance's mouth dropped open in surprise.

Tinker Bell had changed from an ash-blonde to a red head. Her hair was now almost the exact shade of red as Nance's own.

"Wow!" Cory mouthed. He pushed himself out of the car, waving wildly to capture Krystal's attention.

"Peachy!" Nance muttered to herself. "Even when she looks like me, Cory chooses her."

Krystal saw them and moved in the direction of the car, now adding a sashay to her step that had Cory practically drooling.

Men. Nance thought with uncharacteristic bitterness. She got out of the car to join them. Krystal greeted Nance with a bored wave, her eyes sweeping over Nance's Aston Martin with more than a touch of envy. "Nice car, Friz— uh, Nance," she said, looping Cory's arm in her own.

"Thanks," Nance told her, but she needn't have bothered with the reply. Krystal was already dragging Cory toward the bowling alley, leaving Nance to follow in their wake.

Sugar hadn't arrived yet, so Cory secured a lane for them, picking up a pair of size nine shoes for Nance, and size five for Krystal.

Deciding that animosity between herself and Krystal was ridiculous, Nance determined to try to start over. After all, if Cory had his way, Krystal would become Tinker Bell Miller.

If she wanted to remain a part of Cory's life, Nance had better learn to get along with Krystal sooner rather than later.

"Bowling shoes are the ugliest, aren't they?" she asked Krystal as they removed their street shoes.

Krystal shrugged and used a careless finger to flick back the suspiciously red hair. "I don't know. These don't look all that different from the ones you're taking off."

Nance gritted her teeth. "Uh huh. So, how long have you worked at the Foot Fetish?"

"Two years." Krystal finished tying her shoes and stood up. Bouncing up and down on the balls of her feet, she stretched one way and then the other.

Nance had run out of conversation, so she simply watched her. The girl was serious about bowling.

"Hey guys!" It was Sugar.

He waved, coming down the steps to join them. A pair of bowling shoes dangled on his shoulder, attached to long shoe strings. He carried a bowling bag in his hand. He sat a short distance from Nance and quickly changed shoes. Next, he unzipped his bag and added his personal bowling ball to the array.

"Ready for action," he spoke to both Cory and Krystal. His eyes lifted briefly to Krystal's new hair color, but he made no comment, before turning to Nance.

"Glad you didn't change your mind," he told her.

Nance felt a lightness in her heart. She was glad to see him. "I couldn't let you down, Sugar."

Sugar rubbed his hands together. "All right then, you ready to kick butt?"

"More than ready," Nance answered with a laugh.

"You all heard her. We're going to show you pups how it's done."

"You might have to do the showing on your own," Nance told him. "I'm awful at bowling."

"I'll give you a few lessons."

"Sure," Nance agreed readily.

"We're ready to start when you are." Cory's expression was still reserved.

"I'll help," Krystal offered, earning a surprised look from Nance.

"Won't take but a second," Sugar answered. He rose, taking Nance's hand so that she stood as well. "Most people have trouble bowling because they think it's easier than it is," he told her.

"Really?"

Sugar nodded. "Bowling is a mind game. It's the original hand-eye coordination game." He took one of the bowling balls and handed it to Nance. Leading her over to the lane to which they'd been assigned he told her, "Don't worry about the pins, worry about the path. Your job is to control the path."

He stood behind her. Taking her right hand into his own, he gently moved her hand forward and backward several times.

"You've got it." He said, giving Nance an approving smile when she'd rolled the ball back and forth in a straight line several times. "You want to send the ball out with a nice, easy swing. You don't want to throw it like a baseball. Roll your arm along the path. Drop the ball in the path. The ball will take care of the pins. Got that?"

"I think so."

He was so close. The heat from his body warmed her. His touch was gentle on her wrist.

"Are you guys done yet?" Krystal's strident query shattered the moment.

Glancing back, Nance caught Sugar's gaze. He smiled and Krystal's nastiness didn't seem nearly so obnoxious.

"I think so," he answered for the both of them. "You're ready to go, aren't you, Nance?"

"Let's kick butt," Nance told him.

It wasn't a promise she could keep. True to her word, Nance was an awful bowler. She might have done better if that elusive path Sugar had discussed was painted onto the lane with ten-foot-high guides.

Nance's sole consolation was that Cory was equally deplorable at the sport, something that earned him Krystal's scorn.

"C'mon," Krystal told him after he'd sent another ball flying down the gutter, "you can do better than that."

Sugar, on the other hand, was fabulous. The game really existed between Krystal and Sugar. Nance and Cory were the handicaps. Not that Nance minded. Sugar Smith made being a handicap downright enjoyable.

Each time Nance got up for her turn, he would encourage her. "Come on, Nance. You've got the right stuff!"

If she hesitated, even a moment, he would come behind her and take her arm with his right hand, letting his left hand rest against her stomach. "Just drop the ball into the path. You see the path, don't you Nance?"

"I don't know," Nance told him every time.

"That's okay," Sugar would answer. "You're doing great."

Nance almost believed him. In any event, he said it enough that she actually began to get more of the balls down the lane than into the gutter.

When their team won, Nance could claim to have contributed one strike and three spares to their total score.

"You did great!" Sugar whooped after the last frame. He caught her up in his arms, and spun her around in a circle before planting a loud, smacking kiss full on her lips.

"Thanks," she laughed as he set her down. He gave her one final pat on the back, and then went off to congratulate Cory and Krystal. Nance stared after him, an expression of bemusement on her face. He'd just kissed her, and it was no big deal.

A few moments later, Cory crossed over to her. "I saw that," he said, lowering his voice so that his words couldn't be heard. "Nance, that guy has more moves than a relocation van."

"He's just a nice guy," Nance countered, unwilling to see Sugar's actions in anything but a positive light. "You worry about Tinker Bell. I can take care of myself."

"Normally I would agree with you, but you're not used to guys like that. Guys who sweet talk women into getting what they want. How do you think he got the name Sugar?"

Nance couldn't help herself. She laughed. "I don't know. His mother, maybe?"

"Yeah, like you'd name your kid, Sugar."

"He is pretty sweet."

"You certainly seem to like him."

She couldn't win. Cory was determined to think of Sugar as some sort of fortune hunter. "How are things going for you with Krystal?" She asked, changing the subject.

Cory's transformation was immediate. "I really like her, Nance. She's the prettiest girl I've ever seen."

"Really? I take it you like her as a red head?"

Cory shrugged. "The color of her hair doesn't matter. She looks great either way."

Nance glanced over to where Krystal held Sugar in animated conversation, her hand draped possessively on his arm.

"Isn't that kind of shallow?"

"What?"

"Falling for Krystal based on her looks."

He gave her a look of patent disbelief. "Yeah, Nance. Like you don't notice if a guy is good looking."

"Women aren't like men. They don't fall for a guy based on looks alone."

"Oh, and that blonde model guy on all those butter commercials—the one with the overdeveloped pecs—is a real mutt."

"Fabio? He's an exception."

"Why?"

"Because he's exceptionally good looking. But, he's the stuff of fantasy. The rest of us are stuck in reality."

"So, do you think Sugar Smith is cute?"

Nance shrugged.

"That's not an answer."

Nance walked over to the bench, sat down and began to remove her bowling shoes. "Yeah. I think he's cute. In fact, the way I see Sugar is a great example of what I'm talking about."

"What's that supposed to mean?"

"When I first met Sugar, I thought he was...."

"Scary?"

"Different. Not my type. I judged him because of his style. Twenty minutes later, he became one of the best looking men I'd ever met."

"Oh, really?"

"Oh, really."

"Even though you're supposed to have the hots for me?"

"Why do you keep bringing that up?" Nance asked irritably. "I would think it's something we'd both like to forget."

"I only brought it up because you're acting weird.

"Weird?"

"Weird. An hour ago, you were crying on my shoulder about how much you loved me. Now, you're wrapped up in this Sugar guy—love that name, don't 'cha know. That's weird."

"For your limited information, I haven't changed at all. I'm just getting over a bad case of the 'hots' for a man who doesn't have the 'hots' for me."

"See what I mean." Cory spread his hands outward in a resigned gesture. "Now you're being nasty. The old Nance would have never talked to me this way."

Cory was being deliberately obtuse. "Maybe I should have. Maybe then it wouldn't be so easy for you to take me for granted."

"I don't take you for granted."

"Whatever you want to believe, but lets understand each other. I've spent most of my life making sure I fit to what you wanted. Now that you've got Krystal, I don't have to do that anymore. I have no one to please but myself." Nance lifted one brow and flashed an impertinent grin. "And myself thinks Sugar Smith is about as hunky as you can get without being named Fabio."

She swept up her bowling shoes from the floor and stood. "I'm tired of letting opportunity pass me by. I told you earlier that you were free, but the truth is that you've set me free. Believe it or not, I'm beginning to realize how lucky I am that I didn't get stuck with you after all."

She turned away from him, intent on joining Krystal and Sugar, but he caught her, his grip almost painful on her arm, his voice was choked with emotion. "I'm just trying to look out for you, Boo, like you do for me."

Nance refused to face him. "Don't bother. I'm all grown up, Cory. I have to face the fact that you don't want me. You've made your bed. You've chosen your bed partner, and it's not me.

I only hope your dreams are pleasant ones." Snatching her arm from his grasp, Nance marched away from Cory Miller, and for the first time in her life, she didn't look back.

CHAPTER FOUR

Elsie Morgan, Corance's Director of Marketing for the Midwest region, stuck her head into Nance's office. Her expression was one of scandalized outrage. "Have you seen the new receptionist the temp agency sent over?"

Nance couldn't resist; she sighed and rolled her eyes heavenward. "I've seen her," she said, motioning for Elsie to enter the office. "Her name is Krystal Adkins. And don't blame the temp agency. Cory hand-picked this one himself."

Brows lifted high enough to disappear under the thick bangs of a blunt-cut pageboy, Elsie came into the room and dropped into the chair opposite Nance's desk.

"You're kidding," she said, her eyes full of dismay behind a pair of Ralph Lauren spectacles.

"I wish I were." The opportunity to unload what felt like a truckload of frustration tugged at

Nance. "You know Cory when he gets an idea."

"An idea?" A look of disgust crossed Elsie's face. "That girl isn't an idea. She's a walking lawsuit. She's a bimbo with nothing to recommend her but boob-atude. Oh, and if you haven't seen her this morning, I suggest you take a gander at what fashionable bimbos are wearing for business casual this season."

"Tell me she wore clothes," Nance pleaded, only half joking.

"There's fashion sense, and fashion sins. She falls so far into the latter category, that I doubt she can be redeemed."

"I'll talk to her," Nance promised, rising from her desk.

"Good." Elsie remained seated. Absently, she removed her glasses, using the edge of her salmon colored silk skirt to clean them. "Nance, one other thing." She pushed the glasses back in place, and eyed Nance with a cautious gaze.

"Something wrong?" Nance asked, and resumed her seat, her mind leapfrogging from Krystal to other possible concerns. "You're not having problems with the Inferno campaign?"

Elsie shook her head and smiled. "No problems with Inferno. Sales are actually—dare I say it—hot, especially considering that we weren't first to market."

"Now that's what I want to hear." Nance relaxed. "I haven't seen any numbers yet, so I've been curious. Rolling out the Inferno campaign was expensive."

Elsie shrugged, dismissing the concern. "Inferno will be a best seller for versions to come." She dropped her gaze. "Actually, I wanted to talk about something more personal."

"Oh?" Nance blinked. It was difficult to imagine trouble in Elsie's personal life. From the outside, Elsie had it all, a perfect life. She had a loving husband and three wonderful sons. The boys, ranging in age from seven to twelve, were rambunctious, but they weren't troublemakers.

"I hope everything is fine at home?" Nance questioned, keeping her tone light.

Elsie's airy wave dismissed that fear. "Except for those boys running me ragged, things are fine at home."

"Good." Nance murmured, unable to think of any other problems Elsie might be experiencing.

Elsie wasn't thinking of herself, however. "I don't mean to pry into your personal life," she said after a moment, "but I would like to think that you and I are friends."

"We are," Nance assured her. They didn't

spend a lot of time together outside of the office, mainly because both women were so busy, Nance with work and Elsie with her family. Even so, Nance had always counted Elsie as one of her friends.

"Then, you can tell me to mind my own business, but what's going on? With Cory, I mean. I always thought that you and he. . . ." She hesitated. "Listen, if I'm out of line, just say the word. I'll shut up. It's just, well, I thought you and Cory were a couple."

Even though Elsie's first words gave Nance an inkling of the direction she was headed with her statements, hearing the words spoken aloud sent a wave of sorrow washing over Nance.

She felt as though she were caught in the hold of an undertow, drowning and wanting so much to reach shore. If she could just respond lightly, maybe with a peal of surprised laughter, a disclaimer and a joke about how Cory preferred cartoon characters to flesh and blood women, but she couldn't. The stinging pain of Cory's rejection was too near; her heart was still too fragile.

"We're just friends." Her voice was thick, laced with a heavy sadness. She choked on the phrase. *Just friends.* She'd wanted so much more. Too much, she realized now. She'd been a fool to think that a woman with a nickname like Frizzy Tizzy could attract someone as handsome as Cory Miller.

With a start, Nance realized she was trembling. Cheeks flushed with embarrassment, she met Elsie's concerned gaze. She drew a steadying breath, finding it difficult to speak. She could only hope that Elsie would ignore her obvious discomfiture. "We've been friends forever," she said finally. A following attempt at laughter sounded more like a sob.

It was clear from Elsie's sympathetic expression that she wasn't fooled by Nance's attempted bravado. She was gracious, however, not to comment on Nance's obvious distress. Instead, she reached out and gave Nance's clasped hands a quick, firm squeeze. "Cory will come to his senses," she assured. "When he does, forgive him. Please."

"There's nothing to forgive," Nance answered simply. She'd loved and she'd lost and that was all there was to it. The last thing she wanted was a lynch mob of Corance employees pitting themselves against Cory for her sake.

"Maybe not in your eyes, but I'm just mad enough to give Cory a piece of my mind. It's obvious that he's lost his."

"Cory thinks he's in love with this girl." The words were like daggers into Nance's own heart.

"Love?" Elsie's laugh was incredulous. "Cory might think he's in love with Miss Bold and Beautiful, but he's confused."

"He seemed pretty certain to me."

Elsie shook her head. She, at least, seemed confident that Cory's feeling for Krystal were temporary. "It's that alpha-male thing," she said. "Something must have triggered a deep-seated fear in Cory, and now he's looking for a bimbo to dominate. It's the equivalent of beating your chest and roaring across the jungle. Don't worry, Nance. Cory is far too intelligent to act the fool too long."

"I don't know." Nance shrugged. "Cory seems pretty taken with this particular bimbo."

"Why?"

"Why?" Nance spread her hands in a gesture of helplessness. "She's got the right chemistry. He's the Ying to her Yang. I don't know how she caught his eye. But, I do know that she's what he wants."

Elsie anchored her hands on her knees, elbows pointed outward. Her expression was challenging. "With all due respect, boss lady, if this love fiasco continues overlong, I'll blame you."

"Me?" Nance asked nonplussed.

"You." Elsie was adamant. "If Cory ever gets to the point that he's asking Bimbo number Nine to get hitched, it's a sure sign that you've given up the fight."

"Wait a minute." Nance waved her hands in the air, signaling a time out. "This isn't about me. I'm just an innocent bystander. There is no fight. Cory wants Tinker Bell."

"Tinker Bell?"

"I meant Krystal. What is there to fight about?"

Elsie leaned forward. "Two things, Nance."

"Well, tell me what they are because I've missed them completely."

"Number one, the right for smart women to live in peace and harmony."

"You've lost me."

"Look at Tinker Bell. . . ."

"Forget I called her that," Nance interrupted. "It was just sour grapes."

Elsie shrugged. "Well, it fits. This Tinker Bell of yours is a *bona fide* bombshell."

"She's not my Tinker Bell, she's Cory's Tinker Bell," Nance protested.

"Yeah, well, it depends on your perspective. Anyway, Tinker Bell, TB for short, is a bombshell, a real Marilyn Monroe type, and that's fine with me. I'm normal looking. I've got enough cuties to get by, but not enough to be Miss America. I'm a typical American female, meaning that my situation is reality for most women."

"Your point, if you have one?" Nance arched a curved brow in inquiry, but a smile played about her lips.

"I'm getting to the point. Bear with me. Anyway, so God, in his infinite wisdom, only dumps the *yeah, baby* on a chosen few. The rest of us he's like, 'Look, I gave you brain cells.'"

"Really? I had no idea he was so particular."

"Okay, maybe he doesn't necessarily agree with my assessment of things, but it's what I believe. I actually like this system because it keeps me from getting bored."

"What was that point again?"

"Okay, okay, here it is. There was a time in this great country, if you didn't have enough *yeah, baby* to snag a man, you were out of luck in the success department. I'm serious," she insisted as Nance dissolved into gales of laughter. "My grandmother went to jail so that women could earn the right to use their brains to get ahead. That chickie of Cory's is trying to put us back one hundred years. Well, I'm here to pick up Grandma Katie's banner. If you won't slap sense into Cory

Miller, then I will."

"Uh, oh!" Nance was still laughing. "Should I call Cory and warn him."

"No. This is a women's solidarity thing."

"Krystal's a woman," Nance pointed out.

Elsie snorted. "Yeah. Right. Krystal's a little girl who still thinks the only way to get a man is by showing off the overgrown watermelons on her chest."

"She can't help her looks, Els."

"True. But, she can change the marketing program."

Nance laughed. "So what was your other point?" she asked, when she could speak once more.

"I just made it. You can change your marketing program too."

Nance blinked, caught off guard by the statement. "I don't have a marketing program." She crossed her hands over her chest and tried not to appear resentful.

"Everyone has a marketing program," Elsie returned, her voice gentle with understanding. "In college, I took Marketing 101. Back then, according to the marketing gurus, marketing was all about the medium, *i.e.*, television, radio, print, whatever. Supposedly, according to my wise-guy professor, the medium was the message. Well, that's bunk. The message is the message, and there are a whole lot of messages sent by a person's appearance. You've got other positives beside your brain cells, Nance, but for some reason, you're not accentuating them. Cory is just a man, and sometimes men ignore subtlety."

Nance didn't know what to say. The conversation had been amusing when it centered solely on Krystal. Now, however, it came far too close to the insecurities that Nance kept hidden deep within her. Save-face humor, that was what she needed. "You think I'm too subtle?" She flashed Elsie a lop-sided grin. "I'm sure Cory would disagree."

"Cory wouldn't know to disagree—at least not until you showed him a little flash and dash."

"Flash and dash? I'm too afraid to ask what that means."

"Flash, get your hair done at a good salon. Pick up a little black dress—something tasteful, mind you, `cause we're talking flash and not the trash du jour. Dash, add a little spice to your conversation. Tell Cory he looks good. Tell him he's strong. That's the dirty little secret that men keep hidden from women. They need to hear that kind of stuff, most just won't admit it. Remind Cory that you're not his brother. You're not one of the guys."

Nance was nonplussed at such plain-speaking. "Flash, dash, what comes next?"

"Next?" Elsie's smile was secretive. "Why don't you test the advice and find out."

Nance shook her head in mock despair. "I think I'll pass. But, you could have told me this stuff sooner, Elsie. Why didn't you?"

"Because I had no idea that Cory was so blind to what was right in front of him."

Nance's lips turned up in a wry grimace. "Now you're talking. By the way, that bonus you're angling for is in the mail."

"Good, I deserve one," Elsie grinned and rose from her chair. She moved over to the door where she stopped and faced Nance again. "You know, a real bonus would be for you to take my advice."

Nance considered the statement. "I just think it's too late. It would be humiliating to chase after Cory when he's clearly not interested. But I appreciate your honesty."

Elsie nodded. "The thing about true love is that, sometimes, it requires that we make absolute fools of ourselves before it hands over the grand prize."

Nance wanted to believe, but she'd already

played the fool for Cory—many times. A haircut and a black dress wouldn't make a bean's worth of difference in his feelings for her. He'd been more than clear on that point. He could never love her the way she wanted. It was something Nance had to accept.

There would be no trips to the hairdresser, no makeovers to get Cory's notice. If Nance was going to make any such effort, it would be for herself, not for Cory.

"Thanks, Elsie," she said. "I'll think about it." Maybe she'd get a makeover before attending Cory and Krystal's wedding.

Elsie firmed her shoulders, accepting defeat. "You do that. Meanwhile, I'm off to beard the dragon in his lair. Wish Cory luck."

Nance shook her head. "I would, but my sympathy is with you. Knock him dead, Els."

Elsie saluted, and bursting with purpose, marched from the office, leaving Nance alone with thoughts too disquieting to permit a focus on work.

A makeover.

It was laughable.

Cory would think she'd really gone off the deep end. And he'd be right. Elsie meant well, but Cory's decision was made. He wanted Krystal, and there was nothing Nance could do about it.

In the meantime, they'd make the best of an uncomfortable situation.

The phone on her desk rang. She pushed the speaker button. "Nance Hadley."

"Uh, yeah." An uncertain voice crackled over the line. "This is technical support, right?"

With a sigh of resignation, Nance recalled that Elsie's original complaint had been about Krystal's inappropriate attire. Apparently, there were other problems as well.

"Not exactly. I'll transfer you." She transferred the call and rose from her chair, intending to have a talk with Krystal, but as soon as she'd hung up, the phone rang again.

This time the call was for Elsie. Nance transferred the call to Elsie's voice mail. The phone rang again and then again. It was several moments before she was able to leave her office. In the meantime, she rerouted calls to several different departments.

Finally, she made her escape. Her throat clogged with dread as she considered Krystal's response to a conversation dealing with her attire and with her need for more training. Still, it had to be done, and Nance was the one who would do it.

The reception area was located some distance

from Nance's office. As she moved up the long corridor to the front of the building, Nance mentally rehearsed what she would say to Krystal, but the carefully worded speech vanished like water on a hot day when she saw Krystal seated at the reception desk.

Feet shod in a dainty pair of Night Dreams and crossed on top of the desk, Krystal wore a plain gray T-shirt stretched so tightly across her generous chest, that it left little to the imagination—including the brand name of her underwear.

A true BARB, she'd paired the shirt with a pair of ancient jeans sporting twin rips strategically located in the seat.

She was on the phone, a personal call from the sound of it. When Nance appeared in the room, Krystal whispered into the phone. "I've got to go. The bride of Frankenstein is here. Yeah. I'll call you later."

Nance looked around the reception area. There were at least four people waiting. Ignoring Krystal, she greeted the person closest to her.

"Hi, can I help you?"

The man was furious. "I've been here for thirty minutes waiting for an appointment that should have begun forty-five minutes ago."

"I apologize." Nance flashed a heated glance

at Krystal, but knew better than to make excuses to a client. "Who were you scheduled to meet?"

"Cory Miller."

"If you'll wait a moment longer, I'll inform Mr. Miller that you're here."

The man sat with a hrumph. It was clear that he'd already made up his mind about Corance software based on the behavior of the company's staff.

Nance went to the next person. "How can I help you?" she questioned, now dreading the answer.

"Waiting for a signed contract to return to Capital Investments."

Nance directed him to the legal department. There were two others waiting, and within the space of five minutes, Nance had dealt with everyone.

Too angry to even speak, Nance returned to her office. It didn't matter how knee-deep in heat Cory was, she had no intention of allowing him to run Corance Software into the ground—especially not for the purpose of impressing a BARB. They'd both worked hard to build Corance into a successful company. Nance wasn't about to throw it all away.

She picked up the phone and quickly made a series of calls. A short time later, her phone calls complete, Nance returned to the reception area to find Krystal reading a comic book.

She closed her eyes and counted to ten.

"You wanted something, Frizella?" Krystal asked without looking up from her book.

Expression grim, Nance leaned over and stripped the book from Krystal's grasp.

Somehow, Krystal had gotten the erroneous notion that Nance Hadley was a pushover. And maybe she was, where Cory Miller was concerned. But enough was enough.

"Yes, Krystal." Nance met Krystal's outraged gaze with a deliberate stare. "I do want something."

Laurie, the relief receptionist, chose that moment to make a timely entrance.

"Krystal, this is Laurie. She will be taking on your duties for the rest of the day. I'd like a word with you in my office."

Finally, Nance caught a flicker of concern in Krystal's eyes, but it was brief. Krystal shrugged her shoulders, retrieved her handbag from the bottom drawer of the desk and said, "Show me the money, girlfriend."

Nance ignored her, and turned instead to Laurie who was already handling the ringing phones with business-like proficiency. "Thanks," she mouthed silently.

Laurie nodded.

In grim silence, Nance led Krystal to her office, where, rather than showing concern, Krystal paced the perimeter of the office, nodding her head as she studied the various pictures and awards placed on Nance's wall.

"So, this is where the high-lifes hang?" Her voice was full of insolence.

Nance plopped down in the seat behind her desk. She'd been hoping for some sign of remorse—anything that showed Krystal cared about her job. This lack of concern only strengthened Nance's resolve. Krystal was about to get a wake-up call.

"I don't know about high-lifes." Nance steepled her fingers together before her. "But, I do know that Corance doesn't employ low-lifes."

Krystal turned from the photo of Nance and Cory at the ribbon-cutting ceremony for the Corance offices. Challenge glittered in the depths of her gray eyes. "What's that supposed to mean, Frizzy?"

Nance didn't bother hiding her frustration. "It means your performance level is disgustingly low. We have a dress code here, Krystal. Our dress code is business casual, which means you can wear nice slacks, not jeans that look like they belong in the garbage heap. When clients walk in the door, those clients should be greeted with a smile. Their needs are top priority for our staff. That's why you get paid."

Krystal's eyes narrowed to slits, but before she could speak, Nance continued.

"And, lest I seem unfair, please know that you don't have to like the job. However, if you don't like it, then don't do it. You know the way out of the building, just don't let the door slap you in your rear on your way out to find something more suited to your liking."

"Look, I didn't want this job," Krystal snapped back, her eyes flashing with dislike. "You came after me, Frizella, not the other way around."

Abruptly, Nance stood. Balancing balled fists against her desk, she said, "That's where you're wrong *Barbarella*. I didn't come after you. Cory did. I was roped into being the messenger. Even so, I'm not going to roll over and play dead while you tear up my company with your over-manicured claws. If you want to keep this job, you'd better get a quick clue about proper business behavior."

Krystal shrugged as if she couldn't care less. "And I suppose you intend to give me a clue."

Nance sighed, the anger leaving her as quickly as it had come. "I'd be happy to help you, Krystal. Lesson One: Lose the attitude. This isn't high school. No one appreciates your tough girl act."

"Fine. Anything else?"

Krystal was listening. Nance could see it in her defensive posture. She felt a surge of triumph. "Lesson Two: My name is Nance Hadley. You can call me Nance. Call me Frizella again, and you're asking for trouble."

"Fine. Can I go now?"

"No." Nance came around to the front of her desk and perched herself on top. "Lesson Three: One of the benefits that Corance extends to our consultants is a clothing allowance. Elsie Carlson will be taking you shopping this afternoon. Don't return to Corance without decent attire. Elsie will be happy to show you what decent means."

"Fine." Krystal crossed her hands over her chest. "I'm sorry. I didn't know you people had all these rules."

"We do have rules, Krystal." Nance could afford to be magnanimous. Krystal wasn't the rebel she pretended. Deep inside, she was more a scared little girl.

Nance was surprised by a feeling of compassion towards Krystal. "The rules are supposed to make life easier for our employees and our customers." She leaned back and pulled an employee manual from her desk drawer. Holding it out in Krystal's direction she said, "Please scan this. You don't have to know it word for word, but you'll find that most really good companies have a strong corporate culture. We've spent thousands of dollars to develop a work style. People who don't fit that style usually don't survive long at Corance. Your hiring was done differently. And I think it's safe to say that Cory and I bear a great deal of the blame in this situation for not communicating better. The manual is also on the company intranet if you'd rather look at it there."

Grudgingly, Krystal reached for the manual. "You're not just picking on me cause you have a thing for Cory, are you?"

Nance inhaled sharply. "I would never do that."

"I know how you feel about him." Krystal's voice was more confident now. "I can see it in your eyes."

Nance rose and returned to her seat, placing the desk between herself and Krystal as though it would provide some form of protection. She stretched clasped hands out before her and considered how best to respond to the girl's obliquely voiced concerns.

Because of Nance's feelings for Cory, it would be all to easy to pick on Krystal. Briefly, Nance examined her motives and knew that in this instance, she wasn't acting out of a desire to get even.

Besides, she was sincere in her efforts to let go of her love for Cory.

"Krystal, you may not have realized that Cory and I have been good friends since grade school. I care deeply for him. I don't want to see him hurt."

"Are you warning me off?"

"No."

Krystal's words came in a rush. "You don't have anything to worry about. Cory doesn't mean a thing to me. I'm in love with Sugar. Sugar loves me too."

"I see."

"I know it might seem funny, him telling you that he'd like to get to know you better, but that's Sugar's way. He's interested in everything and everybody."

"I'm sure he is."

All at once expansive, Krystal continued, "I've been in love with Sugar from the first day I started working at the Fetish, even before that. I told him then I was going to marry him. I will, too. There is no way I'm letting anyone or anything get in the way of my marrying Sugar."

"What if Sugar doesn't agree with you?" Now why had Nance asked that question? It wasn't like she really cared about the answer.

"Then, I'll make him."

"How do plan to do that?"

"I don't know, but I will."

An odd suspicion formed in Nance's mind. "Are *you* warning me off?" she asked, a sense of amazement lifting her brows.

"Absolutely."

Laughter bubbled up inside of Nance. She pressed her lips together to hold it inside, but she couldn't resist a relaxing of her lips into a tiny smile. It was absolutely incredible that anyone, especially someone as beautiful as Krystal Adkins, could be jealous of Nance. "Krystal," Nance spoke after a moment, "these threats have to stop. I don't know where you grew up, but this is business. You don't survive in business by flashing your claws at everyone you meet." Nance stood, "Besides, I've already given up one man for you. Don't expect me to give up another."

"I guess I'm not the only one with claws," Krystal remarked in a nasty tone.

"No, you're not. You'd be surprised at how

long it takes me to sharpen mine each morning. I've whipped mine out against both men and women, most of them a lot tougher than you."

Nance picked up the phone. "Just a minute," she told Krystal as she dialed. "Elsie, this is Nance. How did it go with the dragon?" She paused, listening to Elsie's answer. "I'll take care of that. Maybe I can get through to him. Listen, I've got a special project that I need you to work on this afternoon. I'm thinking it will take about four hours."

Nance glanced at Krystal, noting the girl's mutinous pout and folded arms. "I'll explain it when you get here, but I think you'll enjoy it. See ya in a minute."

She hung up and faced Krystal. "It makes no difference to me whether you stay at Corance or go back to the Foot Fetish. That's your decision. But if you're going to stay here, you'll do it on the terms that we've just discussed."

Krystal gave Nance a jerky nod, but didn't speak.

"This is your opportunity to back out, Krystal."

"I know what you're trying to do," Krystal snapped. "You're trying to keep me away from your precious Cory."

Nance lifted a bored eyebrow. "I may not be

as pretty as you are, Krystal...."

"You don't even come close," Krystal interrupted. "It won't take Sugar long before he realizes it."

"As I was saying," Nance continued as though Krystal hadn't spoken, "I might not be as pretty, but looks aren't everything."

Krystal placed a hand on one hip, her attitude belligerent. "Yeah. That's what they say. Only they usually say it to ugly girls. Keeps the suicide rate low when the bow-wows start realizing that women like me own the world."

Open-mouthed, Nance stared at the girl. Was Krystal really so vain? Or was she just striking back at Nance for her admittedly provocative comments?

"Believe what you want," Nance answered.

"I will." Krystal held on to her belligerence. "I've heard all the sayings: Beauty is as beauty does. Beauty is only skin deep. Charm is deceptive and beauty fades. But the truth, Nance, is that men fall for a girl based on her looks. That's what happened with Cory." She flicked a lock of wispy blonde hair back from her shoulder and eyed Nance with a superior pity. "Cory wanted me so bad, he was drooling on the shoes. I could have asked for the keys to his mansion, and he'd have given them to me."

"More the fool, he," Nance noted.

"The only reason guys marry ugly girls is because they can't get a good-looking one. So they settle. But Sugar Smith doesn't have to settle. I want him."

Nance had had enough of the belligerence, the vanity, the drama. "If you don't want Cory, don't string him along. Let him know that he doesn't have a chance."

Krystal smiled, and Nance realized that all the girl had wanted was to get a rise out of her.

"You'd like that, wouldn't you?" Krystal smirked.

"I don't want to see Cory hurt. He's a good man, and he really cares about you."

"I'm not a jerk. I've tried to tell him that I'm not interested. It's not my fault he thinks his money is going to change my mind."

"Why'd you accept this job, then?" Nance had to know. "It only takes you away from Sugar." The logic seemed unassailable, but thus far, Krystal Adkins had an explanation for everything, no matter how kooky it was.

"Sugar made me mad, acting like he was all into you. I took the job because I want him to see that I don't need him. I want him to miss me. It's the oldest trick in the book, but a man will fall for it every time." She gave Nance a wicked smile. "I've got this job. If I want, I can have Cory Miller, too. Competition is a powerful aphrodisiac."

"Uh, yeah." The girl was three-and-a-half quarts short of a full gallon.

Krystal continued, "My plan is working, too. Sugar came with us when we went bowling."

It would be a waste of time to point out that Sugar had come because of Nance. Then again, who knew what was going through his mind, but he certainly hadn't seemed all that concerned about Krystal.

The only response that Nance could make was to restate her earlier point. "Cory is a good man. If you're not interested, you should tell him."

"You tell him. It won't change anything. He's convinced himself that he's in love with me. Besides, if Sugar doesn't come around, I might take Cory up on more than his job offer."

Nance didn't have a reply. Thankfully, she was saved from having to think of one by a knock on the door that was followed by Elsie sticking her head into the room.

When Elsie saw Krystal, a huge smile appeared on her face. "My special project?" she asked Nance.

Nance nodded.

"You don't have to act like I'm not here," Krystal put in rudely.

"You're not here, kid," Elsie told her. "That's the problem. You're stuck in some adolescent time warp. But don't you worry about a thing. Auntie Elsie is going to change all of that. When I get through with you, you might just look good enough to marry the CEO."

She gave Nance a thumbs up sign and bustled Krystal from the office, talking all the while.

Nance rotated her chair to face the window. After several moments, Elsie and Krystal emerged from the building. Elsie was still talking.

As Nance watched them leave, she couldn't help but wonder how Cory had managed to fall for someone as flighty and illogical as Krystal Adkins.

But he had.

And Nance would have to learn to accept it. She *had* accepted it, she corrected herself. It didn't matter what Krystal thought; Nance knew that Cory would win Krystal in time. Cory had so much more than money to offer a woman.

He was good looking, charming, smart. He was everything a woman could want.

In time, Krystal would see that. In time, she

would come to love Cory the way Nance did. And Nance would know that she had done everything possible to help them. Her conscience would be clear.

Somehow, the thought didn't bring her any joy.

CHAPTER FIVE

Thank God! The day was finally over. More weary than she could even remember, Nance made her way from the garage in through the kitchen of her lakeshore home. Pausing before the granite-topped kitchen's center island, she gazed beyond to dining room and the trio of nine-foot arched windows overlooking her own private lake, Lake Bennington.

It was a beautiful sight, one that never failed to revitalize her. Today, the view was especially stunning as the summer breeze swept the rolling waves into tiny crests of foam, and the late-evening sun reflected orange rays in a thousand glinting sparks upon the water.

Tonight, however, for all the breathtaking beauty of the view, it wasn't enough to drain the tension leftover from a thoroughly frustrating day.

Nance sighed and turned from the scene. She

would need something more powerful. She dropped her purse on the island and began disrobing, stripping clothes from her body. Shoes ... blouse ... fell to a heap on the floor like layers of shed skin. Then skirt ... slip ... nylons ....

Clad only in bra and panties, Nance padded over to the stereo intercom and flipped the knob over to the jazz station.

Finally, she released her mass of electric hair from its puffy bun, shaking it out over her shoulders with a sigh of relief.

It was a start. Still, after the day she'd endured, she deserved her world-famous strawberry-coconut smoothie, and she deserved it served in her special occasion *Moser* antique crystal.

This was her reward for not going stark-raving mad.

In fact, she deserved more than a smoothie. She deserved a long, hot bubble bath and the Pulitzer Prize for Peace.

The bubble bath she could do. The Pulitzer Prize, well, the committee would never understand the depths of patience she'd had to plumb to resist declaring war on Cory Miller.

Just thinking about the man set her blood to boiling. Although, in fairness, she had to admit that she deserved what she got for allowing her attraction to him to overrule her common sense. Of course, what she'd gotten was Krystal Adkins, a woman who was quite possibly the worst employee on the face of the earth. And the only reason Krystal was employed at Corance was because Nance had given in to weakness.

Well, she was paying for that weakness. The sixty-five-dollar pair of shoes was just the beginning.

Now Corance would be footing the bill for Krystal's new wardrobe—a perk usually reserved for its high-billing technical consultants. Moreover, there was probably no way to calculate the lost revenue from the two hours Krystal did spend on the job. During that time, she'd managed create disasters that had taken Nance all day to repair.

Nance had called a brief status meeting with Cory to discuss the matter, but rather than giving her statements the consideration they deserved, he'd given her a knowing grin. It was clear to Nance that Cory thought her complaints were motivated by jealousy.

"She'll come around," he'd told her. "Cut her some slack. It's her first day."

"I doubt we can afford a second day," Nance had responded tartly, but after that, she dropped the matter. If Cory was unwilling to listen to her input, then she would think seriously about selling her shares in the company. Perhaps she would even start a competing firm. There was no doubt in Nance's mind that she could find the necessary talent to get her own company off the ground. Normally, hiring good employees was her specialty.

For the moment, however, she pushed aside the depressing thought. Things weren't quite to that point yet. Besides, she didn't want to spend the evening mired in the day's events. She would need every ounce of relaxation that she could squeeze from the evening because tomorrow Krystal would be returning to work.

Concentrating on preparing the smoothie, Nance dropped a cup of the frozen strawberries into the blender, added a liter of Crystal Light and an entire can of coconut milk before flipping the switch and setting the machine into whirring motion. Pulling a chair from the dinette, she dragged it over to the cabinet and used it as a step up to the counter.

She rarely used the *Moser*. She'd bought them through an on-line auction last Christmas. At nearly three hundred dollars a stem, she didn't want to run the risk of breaking even one. But tonight, she felt she deserved a reward—even something as small as drinking from antique crystal.

Just imagining the evening she had planned, she began to smile, finally feeling the cares from the day leave her. She'd add the Africa spa bath salts in her bubble bath, and maybe get in some reading as well. She hadn't had a chance to read the new Tess Gerritsen medical thriller, and reading about someone else's troubles might take her mind off of her own broken heart.

Nance climbed onto the counter and stood up to reach the top shelf where she kept the stemware. As she reached for a glass, she was startled by the sound of a strangled exclamation behind her.

Whipping around, she found Cory standing in the doorway of the kitchen, a stunned expression on his handsome face.

"What are you doing here?" she gasped, arms flying down in an effort to shield herself from his view.

"I let myself in," he answered in a bemused voice.

Nance was far too embarrassed to even wonder at the strangeness of his tone. She addressed him with a spunky belligerence. "Well you can let yourself out. Can't you see I'm not dressed?"

Cory grinned and remained where he was, his eyes roaming Nance's figure with distressing thoroughness. "Oh, yeah. I can see that."

Nance shifted her arm so that it provided a narrow covering. "I mean it, Cory." She lifted the glass menacingly. "Your lecher act is not funny right now. If I have to break my *Moser* on your head, I'll do it. Then I'll sue for damages."

Cory lifted his hands in surrender. "Chill, Boo. I'm not going to ravish you. I'm just adjusting to the changes that have occurred since sixth grade. Remember? Your mom said you were upstairs reading, but you were changing clothes . . . ."

"Can we reminisce later, please?"

Cory lifted his lips in a one-sided grin. "If you insist. I'll run upstairs, grab your robe, and be right back."

"Finally, some courtesy," Nance snapped, hoping the blush that heated her cheeks hadn't spread across the rest of her.

Deliberately, he turned his back before replying. "Nance, if you knew what a great body you had, you'd understand that I completely forgot myself."

"I don't care what you forgot," Nance answered crossly. "If you tell anyone that you saw me this way, I'll deny it."

Cory chuckled. "Hey, when a man finds a woman with a figure like yours, he keeps that woman all to himself."

"You wish!"

Cory's reply was lost as he headed up the stairs to retrieve her robe. He returned shortly, backing into the room, Nance's gold crushed-velvet robe in his right hand. He held it just out of her reach, saying, "Since I'm not allowed to look, you'll have to take it from me."

Nance snorted. She carefully placed the *Moser* goblet on the counter and hopped down.

"You made up that sixth grade story," she said, her tone conversational. She inched cautiously in Cory's direction, watching him for any sudden moves. She didn't trust him, not one bit. He was a die-hard prankster, and this was the type of situation he loved to exploit, but Nance had no intention of allowing him to get the best of her. "The last time you saw me in anything revealing was at Beth Dean's swim party in high school."

"Oh, I remember now."

Nance couldn't see Cory's face, but he sounded as though he were smiling. "I don't remember the sixth grade story," she said and moved closer.

"You wish." Cory shifted almost imperceptibly.

"Well, you don't have to make all this fuss."

"You've changed a lot. There are some new. developments. I'm just pointing them out." He took a full-sized step toward the kitchen door.

"Cory . . ." Nance's tone held a warning note.

"What?" His voice was silky with innocence.

"Don't play games!" Nance lunged forward as she spoke the last word, snatching the robe from Cory's grasp.

She'd made her move just in time. A split-second later, Cory was leaping forward— empty-handed.

Laughing, Nance quickly shrugged herself into the robe. "I knew I couldn't trust you to behave."

Cory heaved a dramatic sigh, taking his loss good-naturedly. "You wouldn't like me if I did."

"Yeah? Try it sometime, you might be surprised." She tied the sash into a huge, floppy bow. "You can turn around now."

"All decent?"

"As much as can be expected."

Cory turned, his eyes sweeping over her in a quick examination. "Too bad."

"That depends on your perspective."

"Exactly." Cory wandered over to the intercom system and turned up the music. Anita Baker was on singing "Sweet Love."

Cory joined in, singing with her as he moved toward Nance with purposeful steps. "'With all my heart, I love you, Baby.'" His voice was deep and melodic, blending in smoothly with the professional control the singer exerted over her own notes.

"Dance with me!" He caught Nance in his arms, ignoring her laughing protests. Pulling her close, he swayed back and forth against the sensuous rhythm of the love song.

"Cory, stop it!" Nance said when his arm tightened around her. Her robe offered little protection against dips, dunks, and any other feat of convolution Cory might want to try.

Ignoring her pleas, Cory swung her in a wide arc, whirled her back, and then down into one of the deep dips that she'd feared. He was still singing, "'I'm in love. Yeah, I'm in love . . . How sweet it is, hey!'"

At last, the song drew to a close. Nance waited for Cory to laugh and release her, but he didn't.

Uncertain, she met his gaze and saw blue eyes colored by desire. Fear, mingled with an answering passion, spiked inside her.

I want to kiss you, his eyes told her.

And yes, she wanted that too, more than anything, but her heart was too wounded. There was too much pain between them.

"Please," he whispered, his voice so soft, she almost thought that she had imagined it.

"Yes." Nance was barely aware that she'd spoken the word. She only knew that she had surrendered herself once again to the man who had broken her heart.

Everything else faded — the music, the whirring of the blender, and as Cory drew her back into the warm circle of his arms, even the fear abated. Nothing existed but the two of them. They were set apart in a world where awareness meshed with need and flamed into a raging inferno between them.

Cory's breath, labored from the exertion of dancing, fanned her neck as he pulled her to him. Then he was kissing her, their lips meeting in a renewal of the slow motion dance begun earlier in jest.

It was a kiss that shifted and swayed—that held, released, and held again.

His touch was exquisitely tender. One hand supported her weight while the other cupped her chin. Gentle fingers roamed the hills and valleys of her face in a timeless rhythm.

So sweet.

So perfect.

So right.

What about Krystal? The unwelcome thought intruded itself on Nance's desire-tinged awareness. She drew back in half-hearted protest.

Cory responded by pulling her even closer to him. She was encompassed by the heat of him, by the spicy scent of his cologne. She was teased by a surging swirl of emotion that bid her to put away reason.

Unable to resist, she surrendered to the sweet tumult of passion. Abandoning the last ties of sanity, casting off the last of clinging reserve, she lifted her lips, joining him wholeheartedly in this dance.

As if sensing her acceptance, the kiss changed. Cory's lips moved with an urgency now, drawing a heated course downward along her neck.

Nance groaned.

This was her secret dream, springing to life at last. Cory's heated touch, his hands roaming her, igniting fires of pleasure as they skimmed in wanton passage against her skin.

He walked her backward until she was pressed against the counter.

"Cory," she moaned his name, lost in sensation, lost in the heady freedom that allowed her to express her love for him.

So sweet.

She was carried aloft on feeling, propelled by an upward spiral of emotion. "I love you," she whispered, and felt free, truly, truly free.

Abruptly, Cory broke off the kiss.

The upward spiral turned, spinning crazily out of control.

Puzzled and afraid, Nance opened her eyes. "Cory?"

Awkward now, he disentangled himself from her arms, separating himself from her. She was losing him again.

No.

Come back.

The words stuck in her throat. She knew from experience to speak them would only push him further away. Although, why would it matter? He was already far beyond her reach—much too far for them to regain the precious treasure of a simple friendship. Nance was stung by the blinding realization that he always had been. Only her own foolishness had allowed her to ever believe otherwise.

With a shaking hand, Cory drew a path through his hair, adding to the disarray that Nance had created with her impassioned touch.

"Nance...." He started and fell silent. But he didn't have to speak. His actions spoke in volumes.

Coldness rushed over Nance, followed by the most agonizing pain she'd ever imagined.

This was the final rejection.

There would be no coming back, not after what had just happened between them, and now he was looking for a way to tell her.

Hating herself for even wanting to come to his rescue, she gave him the excuse he needed. "It's Krystal, isn't it?" Her voice was unnaturally high.

He wouldn't look at her. "I'm sorry," he said.

Sorry? She laughed — a shrill, high-pitched sound that bordered on hysteria.

He was sorry? Cory Miller didn't have the faintest idea what it meant to be sorry, but Nance did. She was sorry she'd ever wasted one moment caring for him. She was sorry she'd ever laid eyes on him.

Anger and violence collided in her breast. Uncontrollable tears crowded her eyes, washing across her vision in torrents. Suddenly, she couldn't bear to be the mature one anymore. She couldn't stand to keep her feelings hidden like they were something of which she should be ashamed.

"Out!" She yelled, pushing him, acting on the violence inside her. "Get out!"

Cory intercepted her arms, and instead of moving away, he pulled her to him in a pacifist embrace. Sorrow lined his features. "Boo, I said I was sorry."

Her expression was carved from stone, her tone brittle. "Don't touch me."

"C'mon, Boo. You've got to let me apologize."

Violently, Nance shook her head, sending the red frizzed hair swinging around her like an ion shield.

"I don't know what came over me," Cory continued. There was genuine regret in his tone. "I saw you, standing there. Your body. . . you've got a beautiful body, Boo. I mean, I'm just a man. I guess I stopped thinking. I didn't mean to hurt you, sweetheart. I really didn't."

"That's a cop-out, Miller, and you know it."

"Maybe it is a cop-out. But, I don't want to hurt you."

"Yeah, right," Nance hiccuped. "You never mean to hurt me, but somehow you always do."

"And you always forgive me. Forgive me this time. Please, Nance."

Her tears had slowed, but the bitterness remained, growing like a virulent weed inside her heart. "Forgive you? No, Cory. I hate you. I absolutely hate you."

Remorse angled his lips downward. "I deserved that."

"You deserve worse than that. How could you kiss me that way, knowing how I feel about you? It's cruel."

"I don't have an excuse, Boo. If I say I forgot myself then it makes me a jerk, but that's what happened. I can't explain it, not to you, not even to myself."

Nance took a deep breath. She needed a moment to compose herself.

In a daze, she moved over to the blender, suddenly realizing that through all of the passion, and now the tumult, it had been on. The fruit was completely invisible, beyond being overblended. It had been chopped into nothingness by unrelenting blades and too much time in a blender.

Nance felt the same way. For too many years she'd followed Cory like a piece of fruit caught in a blender, tossed around and around in the same pattern until she wondered if all that existed of her was the nothingness created by Cory's cutting blades.

Well, no more.

He could apologize all he wanted, but she was

done. No longer would she allow him to whip her apart.

Her resolve firm, she faced him. "Look, Cory. Let's just forget this whole thing ever happened. I understand what you're saying. It was heat of the moment." She gave him a brittle smile. "You know, I got caught up in it too. You're not such a bad kisser, Miller. Still, we can't have stuff like this happening. If you're going to come over, then you need to call first."

He frowned. "We usually get together after work."

Nance laughed. The sound was unnatural but she didn't care. "That was BK."

"BK?"

"Come on, Miller, Before Krystal. Things are different now. You're in love with the Boob Queen. Far be it from me to stand in your way."

She could see the hurt in his eyes, but it didn't matter. He'd hurt her too. Ruthlessly, she forced compassion aside. The only thing that mattered now was her own survival. Loving Cory Miller was killing her. It was time to cut the cord that bound them together. "We're friends no matter what," she managed a perky grin, "but it's time to set some boundaries. I can't allow you to just show up on my doorstep whenever you want. It wouldn't be fair to Krystal."

"I disagree." Cory shook his head. "Things don't have to change. I'll just bring Krystal with me. You, me, and Krystal."

Nance stared at him in horrified shock. "Your circuits must be buggy. Krystal Adkins is not welcome at chez Hadley. Got that?"

He nodded.

"It's enough having to put up with her snide comments at work. I said it before, you're on your own with her."

Cory made as if to speak, but Nance interrupted. "And don't you dare try to make this about me being jealous."

"Aren't you?"

Nance counted to ten, twice before speaking. "I hope you know me better than that. I want you to be happy. It's all I've ever wanted, Cory."

"Then why are you pushing me away? Krystal doesn't have to change things between us."

Closing her eyes didn't shut out the pain that wrapped around Nance in a suffocating cloud. "But she does. How can you expect our relationship to stay the same?"

"Because we'll make it stay the same."

"Spoken like a true man."

"Is that meant to be an insult? If so, it doesn't

stick. I'm am a man. I'm a man trying to save a relationship with someone I care very deeply about. You're treating me like some kind of Neanderthal, but I've always been honest with you."

He had, but that didn't make the pain any easier to bear. Nance looked away from him. There was a relentless quality in his words, a sincerity that made her feel as though she'd cast him as the bad guy in a weakly plotted script.

"You're the one who's so eager to get rid of me," his tone was bitter. "I want to know why. Why are you so ready to chuck a lifetime of friendship down the drain?"

"For you it was friendship. For me, it has always been love."

"You keep talking about love, but if you really loved me, you'd be happy for me. Your heart would find a way to open up to Krystal too."

Nance sighed, there was some truth in his words, but not enough for her to toss all good sense to the wind. She needed the distance between them for her own protection. "I am happy for you. And I'm trying to be a good friend, but I'm not a saint."

"No one's asking you to be a saint. I'm just trying to hold on, Nance." He lifted his hands in a helpless gesture. The movement touched her, but she couldn't allow him to break her resolve. "I'm just trying to hold on," he repeated.

"It's not fair, Miller. It's not fair to me. It's not fair to Krystal. Look, you're the one in love with Tinker Bell. It doesn't follow that I have to be her fan too. Does it?"

"I'm not asking you to be her fan. Just make an effort to like her."

"I've tried. Believe me, I've tried. But Krystal stands for everything I hate. She's like one of those plastic blow-up dolls that men love—all body and no brains. Maybe if she were a different type of woman, I could do it, Cory. But the more time I spend with Krystal, the more I realize that instead of holding on, we have to let go. It's the only way for you to be happy."

Wearily, Cory passed his hands over his eyes. "And you expect me to believe it has nothing to do with jealousy?"

"No, I don't expect you to believe that. But, I hope you'll understand why I feel this way."

Cory pushed his hands into the pockets of his jeans. "From what I can see, you've made up your mind, anyway."

Nance nodded.

"We built a company together, Nance."

"We played with toys together too, but it

doesn't mean anything."

Silent, Cory stared at her, his eyes reflecting hurt and confusion. It took every single ounce of will power that Nance possessed, not to run to him, not to beg him to forgive her.

Nance inhaled, holding the air as a buffer against gnawing uncertainty. Maybe she was overreacting. Maybe she was being selfish. Maybe she really was the jerk.

Cory tugged his keys from his pocket. He pulled Nance's house key from the chain, and stared down at it for several long moments before placing it on the counter.

"Next time, I'll call first." He held her gaze.

"Do that." She felt as if she would break into millions of pieces. *Please God, make him go away*, she prayed silently.

"I'd better go."

"Yeah." Nance smiled the dry, brittle smile that was becoming her signature. "Thanks for stopping by, Miller. I'll see you tomorrow at work."

Cory went still. "Nance, about the kiss."

Suddenly busy, Nance turned away from him. She picked up the *Moser* goblet with an unsteady hand. Taking the blender in her other hand, she poured the smoothie, filling the goblet to the top. "Kiss?" she issued a jarringly false trill of laughter. "I've forgotten it, Cory. You should, too."

She faced him, and sipped from the smoothie, one shapely brow lifted in mockery.

"Yeah." He took a step back, his gaze locked with hers. "Yeah," he repeated.

"Bye, Cory." Where had she learned that bravado? Would she really let him walk out of her life and close this chapter on their uneven relationship?

Could she?

He gave her a half-hearted wave and continued to back away from her, his steps reluctant, his eyes sad.

It was for the best.

She was setting both of them free. The thought gave a jolt to her wavering strength. Grip fierce about the Moser Crystal, Nance held herself firm with superhuman effort.

It wasn't until she heard the gentle click of the closing door, signaling Cory's departure, that she allowed herself to relax.

With great presence of mind, she placed the priceless crystal on the counter. Stepping over the discarded articles of clothing, she left the kitchen and made her way up the long center staircase, turning left at the top of the landing. Her bedroom was at the end of the hall.

A LIFETIME LOVING YOU 139

There, in quiet isolation, she performed the final act of releasing Cory Miller.

She crawled into the huge four poster bed that she'd purchased with the hope of someday, therein, sharing her love with Cory.

And she wept.

CHAPTER SIX

He sent her flowers.

A lavish bouquet of purple hydrangea flanked by statice and forget-me-nots greeted Nance when she arrived at Corance the next morning. She'd come in earlier than normal, hoping to get into the office before anyone else, but the flowers were evidence that Cory must have beaten her there.

Fingers trembling, Nance opened the attached envelope, her breath held deep in her throat as she scanned the words. "You are in my heart... Love, Cor—."

He'd written the words in a bold, deliberate style, the very essence of his own personal nature.

Emotion surged through Nance. Hot tears of sorrow and loss, and that forbidden longing, formed in her eyes. Silently, she cursed Cory for his one act of thoughtfulness.

Leaning over, she buried her face in the blossoms, inhaling the wonderful scent of the hydrangea, her favorite flower, not caring that the blooms were growing wet, watered by her distress.

She'd thought that she was done with crying, having spent most of the night with her face buried in her pillow, wetting it with tears that welled up from some deep, deep reservoir of sorrow.

She'd cried until her throat was raw and aching, and her nose was stopped up with mucus. Finally, at around two a.m., she'd fallen into a fitful dose, awakening several times throughout the early hours of the morning, the tears forming afresh each time she recalled Cory's passionate kisses, and how he had withdrawn when she spoke to him about her feelings.

Finally, unable to bear the loneliness of the huge bed any longer, she dragged herself into the shower, dressed and, ignoring the fact that it was only five a.m., she drove to work.

Her goal was to immerse herself in the minutiae of running a company. Then, maybe she could forget. Maybe she could heal.

But he sent her flowers.

A sound in the doorway caused Nance to turn around.

Cory was there. Embarrassed at her show of

emotion, Nance spun away from him and hastily wiped her eyes before facing him again.

She was surprised to see that Cory looked as bad as she felt. Although he was dressed as neatly as always, a shadow darkened his cheeks, evidence that he hadn't shaved, and the bluish circles beneath his eyes bore testimony to the fact that he, too, had slept very little.

"Hi," he said.

"Hi," she answered.

"How are you?" He took two steps into the room, halting abruptly in front of her.

She couldn't answer his question and said instead, "Thank you for the flowers."

"How are you?" he asked again.

Nance turned her gaze to the window and the sunrise just beginning to show itself on the horizon. She didn't know what she would tell him. The hurt of the last several days was too close. Her emotions were too raw.

"I can't," she whispered. She hadn't expected to find him there so early. She didn't have her shield in place. It was impossible for her to pretend that nothing was wrong.

He was beside her in an instant, reaching for her, bringing her against the warm strength of his chest.

"No!" Nance pushed him away, almost shouting the word. The intensity of her emotion must have surprised him. He released her, staring at her with an expression of concerned alarm.

"What's the matter, Boo?" he asked. "Nance?" he repeated when she didn't respond.

Nance wrapped her arms around herself, retreating.

"Don't touch me!" she hissed, moving away from him to stand by the window. "Don't ever, ever touch me again!" The animosity in her tone was surprising even to her.

In all honesty, she wanted to recall the words, to apologize for the depth of her anger, but she couldn't. Her emotions were so mixed up. She loved Cory. With every fiber of her being, she loved him; but right now, she couldn't stand the sight of him, couldn't bear his touch, certain that if he were to touch her, she would shatter completely.

Cory's hands formed into fists at his sides, but he made no move to reach for her again. "Nance, about last night, give me a chance to explain."

"What could you possibly say that you haven't said already?" Nance looked at him, unable to hide the pain in her eyes. She had tried for so long to disguise her hurt, but she couldn't do it anymore. "You're in love with Krystal. She's everything you want... and... and what happened last night, well.... You said yourself, you're just a man. It was a moment of weakness. I understand that, Cory. I finally get it. You couldn't possibly be in love with a woman as unattractive as I am."

"Now who sounds like a jerk?"

Nance clenched her teeth. There were other words, bitter, angry words that pushed at her. She wanted to spit them out, to wound him, to break him as he'd done her, but it went against her sense of fairness. She wouldn't sink to that. Ignoring the question, she asked, "What are you doing here, anyway?"

"I saw you drive up. I thought I'd give you a chance to see the flowers before I.... I wanted to talk to you about Krystal."

Nance gave him a brief nod, and choosing to misunderstand him, asked, "What do you want me to tell her about the flowers?"

Cory frowned. Before he could speak, Nance snapped her fingers and spoke in a tone laced with bitter jocularity. "I've got it. My dog died. That's it. Why that old mutt of mine got hit by a truck."

Cory's features turned more grim by the moment, but Nance didn't care. She continued, each word dashed out sharper than the previous. "It was all very sudden. I was devastated. And you, being the really great guy that you are, sent me flowers." The smile accompanying the words was all lemon and no sugar. "You, being the really great guy that you are, will make Krystal exceedingly happy. You will give her beautiful kids. You'll never get fat. You won't go bald. Oh, and please let me know if I've forgotten to include something. We wouldn't want to leave out even a one of your many perfections."

"Nance, stop it!" In one step, Cory was behind her. He took hold of her shoulders and turned her to face him.

"Stop what?" Nance questioned tartly. Tears blurred her vision, but she refused to acknowledge them, ignoring those that overran their boundaries and slipped in crooked paths down her cheek.

"Stop playing these stupid games."

"Stupid?" She lifted one corner of her mouth in a patent smile. "No, Cory. I'm not stupid. I'm bitter. There's a difference."

"I didn't say you were stupid." Almost tentatively, he reached out to stroke the curve of her cheek with the back of his hand. When he spoke, it was in a voice she'd never heard before—in a voice that was cracked and full of nervous hesitancy. "What would you say, Nance, if I told you that I messed up?"

She pushed his hand away, refusing to give in to the compelling warmth of his touch. He was talking about last night, and she wanted to forget.

Last night, she was the one who messed up.

She knew he was in love with another woman; yet, she'd allowed hope to flourish in her heart. When he touched her, the feelings she'd vowed to deny had come rushing over her. And once again, she had opened her heart to Cory Miller — her foolishly hopeful heart.

In the end, she'd paid the price.

"I'd say, 'duh,'" she answered his question at last. Balling her hands into fists, she anchored them on her narrow hips and stared at him, her gaze was full of challenge.

He laughed. Then grew serious. "What would you say if I told you that I wanted to make love to you last night?"

A thrill of longing ran through Nance at the words. Ruthlessly, she forced it aside and concentrated instead on fanning the embers of hurt and anger. They were the remnants of heartbreak.

"What kind of fool am I, Cory? I might be plain, I might even be lonely, but I'm not so desperate that I would let you make love to me while pretending that I was someone else."

She drew away from his touch, turning back to the window, and seeing not the sunrise, but the years that she'd poured her heart and soul into building this business with him, because of love.

She was such an idiot!

Cory pulled her back against his chest, and rocked her in a gentle rhythm in his arms. "I wasn't fantasizing about Krystal."

"I'm not Krystal."

"I know that, Boo." He released her and moved around to stand before her.

Nance eyed him skeptically.

"I've never kissed Krystal," he told her.

Nance's traitor heart gave a tiny bump of joy. "Spare me the gory details, please."

"Nance, listen to me. I don't want to kiss, Krystal."

Uncertain, she frowned at him. "What?"

"I'm talking about you and me, and last night."

"There is no you and me, and last night was a mistake. It got out of hand. It won't happen again."

Cory laughed, the sound a deep baritone that raised goosebumps on Nance's arms. "That's where you're wrong. That kiss of yours really packs a wallop, Boo." He lowered his head, his eyes on her, seeking permission to kiss her again.

He seemed so earnest, so different. A week, or even a day ago, it would have been enough. Nance would have allowed him to convince her, but not anymore.

She'd changed. She'd finally given up hope, and somehow, one kiss—no matter how wonderful—couldn't erase twenty-two years of rejection.

Quickly, she stepped back, ignoring the disappointment in Cory's eyes.

"What are you saying?" she asked, not certain she understood.

"It sounds crazy, I know," Cory said. "Crazy to just walk in here and say, I've changed my mind. Especially after all of the times we've talked about your feelings. I stayed up half the night just thinking." He lifted a strand of the frizzed hair and twined it around his finger. "As friends, we'd never shared the type of intimacy we shared last night. Nance, you felt so good in my arms...so right. You belonged there, and I knew then that I was making a mistake with Krystal. My biggest fear was that after last night, you might refuse to even listen to what I had to say."

His words were tempting. But, he'd hurt her too many times. Hadn't she just spent the last several days working to push Cory Miller from her heart—working to set him free because it was what he wanted?

His rejection last night had caused something inside of her to die. She doubted that she would ever again find that sweet purity... that trust born of faith, the hope that had so grounded her in love with Cory Miller.

She loved him in a way that she could never experience with another man, but it wasn't enough.

Not anymore.

Slowly, consciously, Nance backed away from Cory, staring at him with the same wary distrust with which she would regard a poisonous snake. "No."

"No?" He was surprised. She could see the amazement in his heavenly blue eyes. "But you said you wanted us to be together."

"Not anymore."

"Because of Krystal?" His expression was contrite.

"Because of you."

"You're not a woman to hold a grudge." Cory's tone was persuasive. "And, don't tell me you don't love me anymore. It's in your eyes. It's written on your face." He moved closer, pressing in when she moved back, following her until there was nowhere for her to go.

When she was backed against the wall, Cory spaced his hands out on either side of her, effectively cordoning off her escape route. "I love you, Boo. Not a friendship love, not a let-me-stay-the-night love, but real love." He tipped her chin up, forcing her to lift her gaze from the buttons on his shirt. "Sweet love, Nance." The intensity in his stare ignited an answering fire inside Nance. She hardened her heart.

"That's all I'm trying to say." Cory's eyes dropped to her lips.

Nance turned her head, resisting the temptation that he still was to her. "I will always, always love you, Cory." Her voice was strangled and tense. "But I know you don't love me."

"I do, Nance."

"As a friend."

"No. I just told you, that changed last night."

"Because of the kiss, or because I was half-dressed?"

Several moments passed before Cory spoke. "I think that I've always loved you as something more than a friend. That's why I didn't date a lot. I wanted to be with you. And last night wasn't the first time I felt the attraction, but I was afraid."

"Why?" Nance had to know. "What on earth were you afraid of?"

"Who knows. Just because."

As an answer to the question, his response was unsatisfactory. Briefly, Nance thought the matter over, and with a sudden flash of insight, said, "Because I'm not pretty—not like you."

Shame cast a shadow over Cory's beautiful features, and Nance knew she was right. His next words confirmed her suspicions. "I'm sorry, Nance."

Nance covered her plain face, her pale, freckled unattractive face, but after a moment, she dropped her hands. Not everyone felt the same way that Cory did about her looks.

"Sugar Smith thinks I'm one of the sexiest women in the world." She sounded like a child trying to play off one friend against another.

"Sugar Smith?" Cory asked incredulously. "You haven't seen him again, have you?"

"What's it to you?" Was Cory jealous? Nance couldn't believe it.

"I just told you I care about you." Anger weighted Cory's words.

"You didn't care last week. You didn't care when you kissed me the other night in the car."

"It wasn't the same."

"No. It wasn't. I was fully dressed then."

Frustration edged Cory's tone. "I'm supposed

to do the hero thing and deny that I find you physically attractive, right?"

"The gentlemanly thing would be not to mention it at all." Nance shot back.

"Hey, you brought it up. Besides, I never claimed to be a gentleman. I think your body is beautiful." He pulled Nance toward him, his intent clear.

Nance halted him with one hand and then, with trembling fingers, she reached up and unhooked one button on her blouse. "It's not love, Cory."

Cory stared at her, his expression a mixture of amazement and consternation.

Nance didn't care. She unhooked the second button. "You want my body," she said as matter-of-factly as if they were discussing the weather. "It's the same thing you felt for Krystal. Lust. It's just lust. Of course, look how long it lasted with Krystal."

A third button slid from its hole and now the blush colored lace from her bra was revealed.

Nance's shaking fingers reached for the fourth button. Her voice was high and strained. "Women with beautiful bodies are a dime a dozen, though, aren't they? Next week, you'll probably think you're in love with Elsie."

Cory swallowed. His own hands trembling,

he reached out stilling her moving fingers. "Stop, Nance," his voice was hoarse.

"It's what you want." Nance was as calm as death. "I've always given you what you wanted. You can have my body, but not my heart. Not my heart, Cory, not ever again."

Cory pushed her hands away. With gentle fingers, he re-buttoned her shirt. "There's only you, Nance. I've just been too foolish to see it." He brushed a haphazard kiss along the side of her mouth. "Aw, Boo, I've been a jerk, but it's not the first time, and it certainly won't be the last. Give me a chance to make things right. With you. With Krystal. Give me a chance to prove that it's you I love, really love."

"And not just my body?" In Nance's mind, it was a rhetorical question. She didn't believe him, not for one minute did she believe he could make such a complete and abrupt turn-around.

"Besides your body," he amended.

"No. You're Krystal's problem now."

"Krystal was a mistake," he said firmly. "She was my last sown oat. I was afraid, but not anymore. You're mine, Boo. Cory and Nance, together forever. Remember?"

Remember? How could she forget? She'd spoken that phrase so many times only to have Cory change the subject, or make jokes, or worse, withdraw.

How dare he quote the words back to her. How dare he use her dreams as a tool to get what he wanted.

Only this time, he wanted her.

It was too late.

There was no going back to the way things were. The hurt was too deep.

"You're more than a warm body." He spoke the words against her ear. "I'm giving you fair warning, Boo Hadley. I'm gunning for you."

Nance sighed and faced him. "Gun all you want. I've spent the last several days getting you out of my system. You're three-and-a-half quarts short of a gallon if you think you'll be able to weasel your way back into my good graces." Nance's stare was as serious as it was direct. "I'm not crying any more tears over you, Miller." Determination made her voice strong.

In contrast, Cory's voice was low and caressing. "I don't want to make you cry, Boo."

"We're business partners—nothing more."

"Uh huh," he murmured. His smile of agreement was laced with purpose. He captured her chin between his fingers. He dipped his head toward her. "Absolutely." His smooth-timbred voice slipped over her, warming her, teasing her.

"And, there will be no more kissing," Nance insisted firmly.

"I agree," he said. "Completely."

And he kissed her.

CHAPTER SEVEN

Cory left her standing in the middle of the office—eyes closed, face uplifted, and lips still tingling from the incredibly sweet taste of his kiss.

She hated him.

With one kiss, he'd stolen from her every inch of the resolve she'd fought so hard to gain. With a single touch, he'd bound her to him in a hopeless passion that could never be satisfied.

Overwhelmed by longing for Cory's kiss, for the simple pleasure of his caress, for the freedom just to close her eyes and allow emotion-drugged sensation to sweep her away, she thought about going after him, giving in.

So what if his newly found attraction to her was based on the shape of her hips and the size of her chest. What did that matter?

Casual affairs were so cliché these days, who would comment? Most people already thought they were sleeping together. No one would blame her if she just gave in.

Granted, it probably wouldn't last, and it definitely wasn't what she'd spent most her life dreaming of, but wasn't something better than nothing at all?

Of course, she knew the answer was no. It was the noble answer, the answer that condemned her to a lonely existence. But no matter how much she craved Cory's touch, she knew that physical desire alone would never be enough.

Senseless passion was a dual-edged sword. Right now, she wanted to break free from the chains of good sense, but doing so would lead only to more heartbreak. It was something she couldn't bear.

And now, the voice of guilt whispered to her that contrary to resisting Cory, she had been far too eager to give in to him. Carried along by desire, she'd moved from refusal to surrender, all the while maintaining a ramshackle façade of protest.

Hypocrite.

Somehow, with Cory's sudden desire for her, she had become that poor, plain Nance Hadley he thought her to be. Desperate and lonely Nance Hadley ... Nance who'd spent her life pining for a man who was too beautiful to notice someone as dull and plain as she.

The thoughts beat against her. She felt like a butterfly gripped in the shell of a chrysalis, frozen forever into this undesirable, incomplete creature, an object of pity.

And the rub of it was that this was reality. She'd done with fantasy and its seductive lies. For Nance, there never would be a breaking free. There never would be a spreading of her wings in revelation of surpassing beauty.

She was no butterfly.

She was a moth. Dull. Gray. Plain.

And that beautifully handsome Cory Miller, all he had to do was crook his finger and Nance would come running.

No, Nance decided. She wouldn't chase Cory, not anymore. She inhaled, tasting the bitterness of self-reproach.

Never again.

In spite of what he'd said, she didn't belong to Cory Miller. She had no intention of trading her self-respect for a love based only on his miraculous and sudden physical attraction to her.

Nance wanted a love that came from the heart and stirred the soul and covered every living inch of space between them with passion. That was how she loved Cory Miller. She cared too much to accept anything less than the same from him.

It was time for her to do more than let go of Cory. She had to accept that, in his eyes, she would always be plain. If she turned her back on reason now, she would pay in the future. There was no doubt in her mind that the time would come when Cory would expect her to be grateful to him for having enough self-assurance to look past her lack of beauty.

A quiet knock on the door drew Nance back to the present. Embarrassed that she'd not moved even one inch since Cory left her, she quickly made her way over to her desk, and picked up a sheaf of papers.

"Come in." She tried to sound distracted, as though she'd been deeply involved in her work and not wasting her time mooning over a man who would never understand her.

Krystal Adkins—a completely transformed Krystal Adkins—slipped into the room.

Nance stared, unable to hide her shock.

Gone were the ripped jeans and form-fitting rebel T-shirt. Instead, Krystal wore a peach-hued, knee-length sheath over which she'd donned a cropped, eggshell-colored, crochet sweater. She wore a set of pearls around her neck and matching pearl studs in her ears. The tousled blonde hair had been smoothed into a professional-looking pageboy, and, on her feet, she wore a pair of buff-colored flats as staid and boring as Nance's own.

Krystal Adkins had become a dress-for-success role model.

"Krystal, you look wonderful!" Nance finally found her voice.

A brief, self-conscious smile lit Krystal's face, before dissolving into a mixture of defiance and something else.

Embarrassment?

Impossible. Krystal Adkins was too full of vinegar to feel embarrassed about anything, but surprisingly, Nance's compliment sent a red wave across Krystal's face.

"Thanks," Krystal murmured.

"I mean it," Nance said, and realized it was true. She did meant it. At the moment, it didn't matter that the two women were less than friends. Krystal's transformation was so extraordinary, Nance couldn't help but express her enthusiasm.

Krystal's eyes were trained on the taupe colored carpet. "Look. I just . . . thanks—for the clothing allowance."

"Don't thank me. It's standard policy." A

policy for consultants, but Nance had never fully appreciated it as an employee benefit until now.

"I never worked anyplace where clothes were part of the benefits package."

"It's mostly offered by technical consulting firms because we hire kids right out of college. A lot of these kids don't even know what a real business suit looks like. So, the clothing allowance helps with the transition." Krystal probably couldn't care less, but guilt made Nance talkative.

Krystal shrugged, showing a hint of her old attitude. "I didn't go to college," she said in a voice of careful indifference.

Was it possible, Nance wondered, that Krystal's "mad-at-the-world" attitude was the result of low self-esteem? Krystal was just two years younger than Nance, but her world had been so limited. The Foot Fetish demographic might include some MBA's, but more than likely, most of the women who shopped there were women like Krystal. Women who needed men, not because they wanted equal partners to share their lives, but because they needed caretakers. They needed men for financial security because they'd never seen themselves as anything more than pretty faces. Far too often, these women traded their beauty for meal tickets.

And when beauty was gone, what was left?

It was the first time Nance realized that being beautiful came with a price tag.

She always had thought of herself as a victim. Poor, plain Nance couldn't fall back on her looks. Instead, she'd had to develop her other strengths. She'd had to be smart and witty to gain acceptance.

And then there was Cory. If she hadn't been in love with him, more than likely, she never would have learned so much about computers. There were a lot of benefits in being plain; benefits Nance had taken for granted.

A sudden protectiveness of Krystal rose inside her.

What had she been thinking when she joined Cory in his stupid scheme?

She realized now that she hadn't thought of Krystal as a person. To her, Krystal was just a BARB—nothing more than a pretty face and a hot body, a mindless, unfeeling sex kitten.

She'd made the mistake of judging Krystal based on her appearance. Now that Krystal was made over into Nance's image, she somehow seemed more acceptable as a human being. Funny how easy it was to see things more clearly now that Cory was no longer an issue between her and

Krystal.

"I hope you like your new clothes?" Nance asked, pushing the bitter thought away.

Krystal ducked her head in a quick nod. "Yeah. I do. I like Elsie, too. Did you know her grandmother was a suffragette?"

Nance laughed. "It's Elsie's favorite topic."

"She's proud of her grandmother." Krystal's tone was a mixture of defensiveness and fascination. "She said a lot of things about women and the different things they've accomplished." Krystal suddenly seemed to realize that her comments were revealing. "Well. I better get back to the front. Cheryl is training me on using the phone system."

Nance nodded. "I don't know if Cheryl told you, but she'll be here for the rest of the month. You should have had the chance to train with her before being thrown into the receptionist duties. Normally we don't do that type of thing to people."

"No sweat." Krystal inched to the door.

"Krystal," Nance stopped her. "Listen, I want you to feel free to come see me anytime. I'm glad you're working with us."

Confusion flitted across Krystal's features, followed by hesitancy and then a shy smile. "Yeah. Sure. See ya later."

"See ya later." Nance watched Krystal ease herself from the room. She couldn't help marveling at the change in the girl.

It wasn't just the clothing. It was her attitude. She seemed more open. The hostile Krystal was gone.

In her place was a woman who seemed vulnerable, yet so full of potential. And no doubt about it, she was much more likeable than the one with nothing more than boobs and attitude to recommend her.

In her new clothes, Krystal Adkins had confidence. Maybe clothes couldn't change personality, but they could certainly bolster one's self-assurance. Krystal was proof of that. She was glowing so brightly that she lit up the room. That light hadn't been there before today. Seeing it, Nance was glad that she'd put her foot down about the clothes.

Moreover, there was no doubt in Nance's mind that Cory would find Krystal's new look attractive.

What would happen to the sudden interest he'd expressed in Nance then? Would it evaporate like disappearing water on a hot day?

It didn't matter.

She didn't care.

She didn't want the type of love Cory offered.

Several hours later, Nance had managed to immerse herself so thoroughly in project reports, that the ringing of the phone was a shock. She snatched the receiver from its cradle.

"Nance Hadley."

It was Cheryl, the receptionist. "Nance, you have a visitor."

"A visitor?" Nance repeated, her mind still full of numbers and projections. "I don't have any meetings scheduled." She ran a finger along the huge calendar on her desk.

"He says you aren't expecting him."

"He?" That got her attention. "Did he give a name?"

"It's a surprise."

Nance sighed. No doubt this one of Cory's jokes. She'd come out of her office to find him with a silly grin on his face.

She wasn't in the mood.

She made her way briskly to the foyer where Cheryl's desk was located. Cory was nowhere in sight, but the man standing off to one side conversing with Krystal was definitely familiar.

"Sugar?" Nance moved forward, her hand outstretched in greeting. She was surprised to see him. Glad, too.

He thrust a bouquet of flowers toward her, a mixture of wild flowers, explaining, "I figured the flowers would buy me a minute or two of your time."

Nance laughed, accepting the flowers with a murmured, "Thanks."

The gift earned Nance a brief, acrimonious glare from Krystal, but she refused to worry about it. Krystal would realize soon enough that Nance was no threat to her, not with Cory, and not with Sugar.

Besides, she refused to crawl out of the way to make Krystal happy. She wasn't looking for love, but she liked Sugar. There was absolutely no reason that the two of them couldn't be friends.

"What do you think of my new look, Sugar?" Krystal did a slow pirouette.

Sugar studied her, carefully examining both her hair and her new clothing. "You've never looked better," he told her. The sincerity in his voice was unmistakable. Krystal preened under the attention and slanted a triumphant look at Nance.

"I couldn't agree with you more, Sugar." Nance's smile encompassed Krystal as well.

"I can see that working here has been good for Krystal," Sugar observed.

"Like," Krystal interjected pertly. "I don't even miss the Fetish. Who'd have thought I'd end up in a cush job like this?"

"Don't sell yourself short, Krystal," Nance felt honor bound to say. "I think you have great potential."

"Besides, the Fetish is nowhere," Sugar added.

"That's not why I worked there, Sugar, and you know it."

Watching them talk, seeing the sudden tension in Sugar's face, Nance felt as if she were watching herself. How many times had she said words like that to Cory—words which had done nothing but divide them? She couldn't bear to watch Krystal make the same mistake.

"Would you like a tour of our offices?" she asked quickly.

Krystal frowned at her, but Sugar appeared relieved by the suggestion.

"I'd love that."

"You come too, Krystal. Did Cory give you the tour?"

Krystal nodded. "Yesterday."

"Then you can lead us."

"Me?"

"Why not?" Nance shrugged. "I'll fill in any blank spaces."

Krystal's gaze was wary. "Okay," she agreed. "Let's start in technical help."

Krystal nodded again. After letting Cheryl know that she'd be giving a tour, she led them down the hall, informing Sugar, "Technical help is just this room where a bunch of people sit in front of computers and take phone calls from mad people."

"That's close enough to be accurate," Nance laughed. "They help our customers figure out why our software isn't working on their systems. They also do reprogramming when software bugs are discovered. Basically, it's a customer-service function with computer know-how thrown in."

Next, Krystal led them to product development.

"This is where they come up with new revs."

"Revs?" Sugar asked. He looked at Nance, but it was Krystal who answered.

"Revisions, or versions, of the software. There's this thing called Moore's law, that says everything is old after eighteen months, so you have to compete with your own products. They're always trying to make everything old in the software industry. It helps them make more money."

"Well, partially," Nance smiled. "In the software business, if you don't constantly improve your product, you stand a good chance of being pounded by the competition. It helps that most people always want updates, although sometimes newer versions aren't all that improved, but new revs, or versions, are a fact of life in this industry. Companies that rest on their laurels will more than likely find themselves out of the running."

"That's right," Krystal agreed. She looked like a child seeking a parent's approval as she looked up at Sugar.

Nance gazed assessingly at her. Krystal was smarter than Nance had given her credit for. If the girl showed true interest in technology, maybe there would be a better place for her after Cheryl returned from maternity leave.

Krystal led them on to research and development, surprising Nance again with information about the job functions, and even some information about future technology changes. Afterwards, they went to marketing and sales, where Krystal proudly introduced Sugar to Elsie, who gave her a thumbs-up sign. Next they went to the shipping and receiving departments.

Nance was surprised to find that, in most cases, Krystal's knowledge of the departments and their functions was excellent. Either she'd really paid attention when Cory gave her the tour, or Cheryl's training sessions were paying off.

"Great job," she told Krystal. They stopped before Nance's office. "We may have you lead tours more often."

Krystal's smile was self-conscious, her eyes sought Sugar's gaze.

"I'm blown away, pipsqueak," he told her. "I didn't know you were such a quick study."

"Yeah? Well, you know, I'm just doing my thing," she replied in the hybridized hip-hop slang she always used when Sugar was around.

"Right," he said, lifting one eyebrow.

"Want me to walk you to your car?" Krystal asked, her smile hopeful.

Sugar shook his head. "Thanks, but no thanks. The tour was great, Krystal. It's obvious you're going places."

Krystal blushed, clearly pleased. "I'll walk you to the front, then. It's on my way."

"No, you go ahead. I'd like to talk with Nance a little more." His warm glance settled on Nance "You're not busy, are you? I was hoping to take you to lunch."

Nance looked from Krystal to Sugar. Krystal had already begun to glower at her, and Nance had the feeling that whether she accepted the invitation, or not, Krystal would find someway to make Sugar's invitation an issue between them. Even so, she didn't want to add to the simmering conflict. She felt as though she'd gained ground with Krystal, and as much as she enjoyed Sugar's company, she didn't want to be the one responsible for breaking the fragile peace.

Intent on formulating a gracious refusal, she didn't notice Cory until he came up behind her and draped his arm over her shoulders with a casual, proprietary air.

Surprise warring with irritation, Nance gazed up at him.

How dare he treat her like she was his property.

No doubt he believed that, despite her refusal, she would just fall into his arms. Well, he'd spend a lifetime waiting. In spite of Nance's resolution to keep Cory at arm's length, a part of her grew still, waiting to see what he would make of Krystal's new look.

"Wow, Krystal," he smiled, "you look nice."

Krystal shrugged. "Thanks."

Now he would drool. Bitterness edged into sour anger in Nance's stomach. He would gush. He would pant like a dog catching the scent of heat.

Cory seemed to know exactly what she was

thinking; and apparently, he was determined to be contrary. Instead of falling into his panting dog routine, he turned a cool stare to Sugar, greeting him with a barely civil nod.

"Sugar. What brings you to Corance?" Cory's grip dropped from Nance's shoulder to midway around her forearm. He lashed her to him no less tightly than a boat to a ship's dock.

Taking obvious note of Cory's arm around Nance, Sugar asked, "How's it going?" Observing the social niceties that Cory had overlooked.

Warmth of manner obvious, Cory looked down at Nance and smiled. "Good. Thanks. I was just coming to find Boo for lunch."

"Boo?" Krystal's smirk couldn't disguise the hard glint in angry eyes. "As in, 'boo you scare me'?"

"Now there's a good way to get fired," Sugar noted sotto voce.

Nance smiled at Sugar, grateful that once again, he'd come to her rescue. She didn't expect Cory to say anything. In fact, she had grown inured to his lack of chivalry. A fact that made it all the more surprising when Cory removed his arm from around her shoulders, captured her hand and lifted it to his lips. "Boo, as in, so beautiful, I'm scared to let her out of my sight," he murmured the words against Nance's hand.

He was telling Krystal, telling Sugar, even telling Nance that he'd had a change of heart. Nance was the one he wanted.

"Right." Embarrassed, Nance snatched her hand from his. Cory Miller had rocks in his head if he thought she would let him railroad her into falling in love with him or, rather, falling back in love with him. Whatever!

It was time for Cory to learn that Nance Hadley was her own woman. He'd had his chance and he'd thrown it away. Nance wasn't about to look back.

"If we've finished with the comedy hour, you're too late," she took great pride in telling him. In a step, she was beside Sugar. She threaded her arm through his, smiling up at him with friendly affection.

"Sugar has already asked me to lunch." She was a free woman now. She could do what she liked, with whomever she liked. It didn't matter what Cory wanted. It didn't even matter what Krystal wanted. Nance would please herself. "Ready to go when you are, Sugar, honey."

Sugar remained expressionless for the space of a heartbeat, leading Nance to fear that he might back out, if he had to compete against Cory.

But he didn't. He smiled at her. Nance could only hope they looked intimate. He winked and Nance blushed, and for once was glad of the response. He patted the hand that held onto his arm with a death grip.

"I'll have her back in an hour," he told Cory. To Krystal he said, "See ya, slugger."

Then he swept Nance along the hall—a grand exit. Nance dared not look back. Instead, she kept up a running conversation with Sugar, none of which she could remember later. In any event, she knew what she'd find if she did look back—hostility in Krystal's eyes, and amazement in Cory's.

CHAPTER EIGHT

Nance kept up the flood of talk all the way to Sugar's car—a cranberry, late-model SUV with a sun roof.

Unaccountably nervous, and feeling more than a little guilty for using Sugar as an escape from Cory, Nance found that conversation failed her, the spate of words drying up, as Sugar pulled out of the parking lot.

The Corance offices were located on Currell. Sugar turned left out of the parking lot, and then turned left again onto Valley Creek. He seemed content with the silence, allowing it to stretch for several minutes, waiting until they were at the corner of Valley Creek and Radio Drive before asking, "You up for Leann Chin?"

"One of my favorite restaurants," Nance assured him.

The restaurant was a short distance, so within

moments they were pulling into the parking lot, and Nance was saved from having to think up conversation as they moved from the car to the restaurant.

They both ordered the Asian tacos, got their drinks, and Sugar led the way to a table at the rear of the restaurant.

"You don't talk much, do you?" Nance asked after they were seated and had already started their tacos.

Sugar laughed. "I'll talk your ears off after I'm done with this taco. Besides that, I thought I'd give you a break. You looked like you were tired of the battle zone."

A trail of juice from the taco dribbled down her chin. Nance wiped it away with a napkin. "Does it show?" she asked, a frown marring the smoothness of her brow.

Sugar leaned back in his chair, his long legs stretched out on either side of the table. "You're doing just fine, Nance. It's the other two who worry me."

Nance couldn't meet Sugar's gaze. He was wrong, so wrong about her. She wasn't fine. She was a part of the problem. In fact, Sugar was the only blameless one of the lot of them.

What must he think of her?

A LIFETIME LOVING YOU 177

After all, she'd waltzed into the Foot Fetish and hired Krystal Adkins away with barely a thought of ethics. And they all knew why she'd done that. She was Cory's pimp, procuring the woman he thought he wanted.

Humiliation flooded her. She dropped her head so that Sugar wouldn't see the hot tears of embarrassment that gathered at the corners of her eyes. He saw anyway. Reaching forward with a gentle hand, he pushed back a strand of the hated frizz.

"Say, what's this?" He found a clean napkin and offered it to her. Leaning forward, he whispered, "The spices make me cry, too. Let's get out of here."

Mortified at giving in to emotion, Nance nodded. Sugar gathered up both of the trays and dumped the remainder of the meal in the garbage cans, before placing the trays in the shelf on top.

In the car, Sugar glanced over at her with a mischievous grin. "No more tears and I'll take you to Bridgeman's for ice cream."

Nance smiled in spite of herself. "I don't know what came over me, Sugar." Her throat was still clogged with an excess of emotion. She cleared it self-consciously. "I don't know if I can keep that promise."

Sugar threw his hands up in the air. "I know. I know. This happens to me all the time. I take a woman to lunch, she breaks into tears."

He was absolutely crazy. She had to laugh. "Thank you," she told him after a moment. "You're just what I needed today."

Sugar's expression grew serious. "Look, Nance, I'm not one to carry tales, but I know Krystal. She gets an idea in her mind, and it's almost impossible to get her to see any other possibilities."

"I've noticed that, too."

"I guess she's taken a dislike to you."

"I think we both know why."

He sighed. "Now I think I'm going to cry."

"She's in love with you."

Sugar tilted his head in a negative motion. "She thinks she's in love with me."

"I don't know. She seems pretty certain."

Sugar rested the tips of his fingers against the steering wheel, a grimace of frustration shadowing his handsome face. After a bit, he seemed to reach a decision. "Let's go get the ice cream, and I'll tell you about Krystal."

Nance nodded her acceptance.

A majority of the stores in Woodbury were new, with everything centrally located in shopping centers. Bridgeman's was a short drive up Radio Drive to the Tamarack Shopping Center.

At Bridgeman's, Sugar chose strawberry ice cream, while Nance selected orange sherbet. They sat in Sugar's car, napkins covering everything, and ate their ice cream.

"So, tell me about Krystal," Nance said between licks. Flashing Sugar a mischievous grin she added, "I know she's got the hots for you."

Sugar shrugged. "Like I said, she thinks she's in love."

"But you don't."

"I don't."

Nance was perplexed by his certainty. "The girl looks at you as if you were a four carat diamond ring. She really likes you, Sugar. She was ready to turn down a perfectly good job offer to continue working at the Foot Fetish. I don't mean to insult the Fetish, but she's making a lot more money now—and no retail hours."

"No, I agree with you. She's better off at Corance."

"She almost didn't take the job because she wanted to work for you."

Sugar's sigh was heavy and heartfelt. "I hired Krystal to work at the Fetish about two years ago." He'd finished his ice cream and now used one of the napkins to wipe at the stickiness on his fingers. "Krystal is— she's got a great look."

"She's a babe," Nance put in, but her tone lacked humor.

Sugar was peeling napkin from his fingers. He favored Nance with a brief, inquistive glance before returning his eyes to his task. "You could put it that way."

He was embarrassed, Nance realized. "What happened?" she asked, her curiosity ignited.

Sugar gave up on pulling the paper from his fingers and rubbed his hands together with an air of serious concentration. Small bits of napkin fell to the floor of his car.

"A Christmas party."

"Oh." Nance understood all too well. The office Christmas party was an occasion at which everyone let down his hair. The company paid for drinks, and usually well-mannered professionals behaved like raving maniacs.

At last year's Christmas party for Corance, Nance had had to plead with Harry Banks, their former director of finance, to leave the stage after he'd got drunk and jumped on stage with the hired band. He'd sung song after song in a loud, off-key voice, and by the time Nance finally dragged him off the stage, he was crying and blubbering into the microphone, begging his wife to forgive him for an affair he'd had with Mary, the head of shipping and receiving.

"I don't want to pry," Nance told him.

Sugar smiled at her. "It's okay. An explanation might make it easier to understand why Krystal reacts the way she does around you. I blame myself. At the time of the Christmas party, Krystal had been employed at the Fetish for about a month. She was a great employee, very sharp."

"And good looking," Nance interjected.

"There was that," Sugar agreed. "At the Christmas party, I worked up the courage to tell her what I thought. She had on this blue dress, looked like a church dress. After that, everywhere I turned, there she was."

"Then someone spiked the punch?" Nance guessed.

Sugar seemed surprised that she understood. "I did." His laugh was rueful. "I spiked it and then proceeded to drink most of it. To this day, I still don't drink the punch at Christmas parties. Anyway, someone brought out the mistletoe, and to make a long story short, the next morning I woke up in Krystal Adkins' bed."

"Wow," Nance said softly. "Just what did you spike that punch with?"

"Nothing that strong. I think several of us had the same idea, and we ended up with more spike than punch."

"So, it's the morning after blues?"

"Precisely. I'm going to let you in on a secret, Nance."

"Which is?"

"Most men aren't superheroes. Most of us are just humans."

"You've lost me."

"I mean, I reacted badly. The last thing I wanted to do was to get involved with an employee."

"You're smarter than some," Nance said, thinking of Cory.

"The whole thing never would have happened if I hadn't been drunk."

"Well, you must have done something right. Krystal still seems to like you."

"After that night, I made sure I stayed away, but Krystal had decided we were a couple. She started making plans. Finally I had to come down pretty hard on her. I told her I didn't want to be involved with her."

"What did she do?"

"She cried. Begged. Pleaded. And then it just stopped. One morning she came to work as normal as can be. I thought it was over, but every now and then she would bring up the subject again."

"You could have fired her."

"No." Sugar shook his head. "The whole thing never should have happened in the first place. If I hadn't been so foolish, it wouldn't have happened."

"Think before you drink, huh?"

He smiled. "Something like that. Anyway, it's a lesson earned and learned."

"For you, but not for Krystal."

"I had hoped that Corance... that Cory, would help her move past what happened. Like I said before, it's been almost two years."

"She won't get over it, Sugar." Nance knew that much from bitter experience. "Maybe to you it was a one-night stand, but I've seen Krystal look at you. She really does love you."

Sugar didn't answer. He stared out the window, his gaze locked onto the sign dually promoting both Bridgeman's and Blimpie's.

"I've been listening to you talk about how Krystal feels about you," Nance said softly, "but it seems to me that you must care for her, too. Otherwise, why are you so concerned? Why haven't you moved on?"

He shrugged. "At the Fetish, we get customers that are so good-looking, it's almost like they're not real. Actually, a lot of them aren't. They get made up, dressed up, doctored up, but on the inside there's nothing. Just a breeze blowing across a desert wasteland."

"Krystal's not like that."

"She's not like that, but what does she want from life? To marry me and work at the Foot Fetish til death do us part? I might have gone for Krystal in a big way, but there was nothing to connect with. Just air blowing across the prairie." He turned to look at Nance. She could see that he was serious. He was sharing a part of himself that he probably kept tightly under wrap most of the time.

"I want to be with someone I can connect with. Someone who listens and hears. Someone who has her own thing going on. I don't want a trophy wife. I'm not into that kind of trip. I want to marry a woman who challenges my mind, makes me a better man."

"What makes you so sure Krystal can't do that? She challenges me."

"I know she can't do that. In the two years she's been at the fetish, she's followed me around like a puppy-dog shadow. If I'm interested, then she is. If I'm not interested, then she's not interested either. If I say the sky is orange, the girl will knock down anybody who says different."

Nance closed her eyes. Did Cory see her the way Sugar saw Krystal?

Was she that way?

Sugar's rueful laugh shook her from self-revelation. "Look, I didn't ask you to lunch for free psychoanalysis." His grin was lop-sided and endearing. "I like you, Nance. That's why I want you to understand this thing between me and Krystal."

"There's a lot between you and Krystal," Nance said in a quiet tone. "Probably too much for you to claim you're a free man."

It was the answer Sugar expected apparently. He nodded and leaned forward to start up the engine.

"Sugar," Nance's voice was hesitant. He looked at her. She leaned forward, aware that what she was doing made no sense. Aware that she was running from her feelings for Cory Miller, rebelling against them... and him.

Slowly, tentatively, she lifted her chin and pursed her lips into a childishly innocent pout.

Their eyes met.

Silent communication heated the air about

them.

In a heart-beat, Sugar closed the space between them, touched her lips with his own, exploring.

Sweet, Nance thought as he deepened the kiss. She opened her mouth and their tongues meshed. He tasted of strawberry.

The flavors mingled, and while the kiss was enjoyable, it didn't make Nance feel the way Cory's kiss did. There was no mind-numbing passion.

Disappointed, Nance pulled back first.

Without her saying a word, Sugar knew. "You love him, don't you?" he asked.

Nance looked away from him, turning her eyes to Interstate 94 and the legion of cars speeding by. She didn't answer.

"If you're in love with Cory, why are you helping Krystal come between you?"

Nance sighed. "What makes you think I'm in love with Cory?"

Sugar slanted a skeptical look at her. "Because you are."

Nance nodded, ceding the obvious. "I'm in love with him. And Krystal is in love with you. Little good it does either one of us."

Sugar chose to ignore the comment about Krystal. "Cory's not interested?" he asked instead.

How could she answer that? Nance pressed the tips of her fingers against her eyes—heart sore and weary. Her only answer was a shaky sigh.

Her lack of participation didn't seem to matter to Sugar. He, apparently, was capable of carrying on the conversation without her.

"Wait a minute . . ." Sugar watched her closely. "He's interested, but he decided this only after putting you through the humiliation of hiring Krystal. So now your pride is hurt." He made it a statement of fact.

"No," Nance was stung into saying. "It's not that simple."

"Your turn then. Break it down nice and simple for me."

"I . . ." She couldn't tell him about Cory seeing her half-clothed. Heat crimsoned her face. That wasn't the true reason she was so at odds with Cory, however. "I don't want him doing me any favors," she said finally.

"Like being attracted to you?"

"Like being attracted to me. I've spent enough time groveling. No way I'm doing it the rest of my life."

She sounded bitter. Heck, she was bitter.

More than that, she was angry. Angry that she was full to overflowing with ugly emotions that seemed more in control of her than she would ever be of them. The realization chipped away at her self-esteem.

Index finger curled thoughtfully over his full lips, Sugar studied her. "Has it ever occurred to you that Cory would be lucky to have you?"

"Not in the slightest."

Sugar shook his head. "You haven't heard a word I've said to you." Tender fingers grasped her chin, turning her to face him. "Nance, I told you before, there's more to love than looks."

"You couldn't prove it by Cory."

"He's interested isn't he?"

"For how long."

"Forever. That's the only kind of love a woman like you deserves."

Her gaze caught his. He was so good to her, a true friend. She wished the passion she felt for Cory could flame to life for Sugar.

"What do you mean?" she whispered the words. The bitterness seemed to rush from her like the sudden breaking of birth waters.

"We talked about it before." His hands smoothed over the frizzy hair, the caring in his caress making her feel beautiful.

"Two kinds of girls, Nance. Remember? Good-time girl. *Forever* girl. The *forever* girl, you don't always see right off. She's hidden. She's our co-worker, our neighbor, our friend's awful sister. You hang out with her. You don't realize it, but you're watching her, getting your questions answered. Is that spark in her eye real? Is that red-hair genuine, or out of a bottle? What's she thinking about behind those sea-green eyes? Is her heart really so deep that she can love someone enough to give him away?"

Nance closed her eyes. His words flowed over her, healing her broken heart, helping her see truths that had always been too shrouded for her to understand.

Sugar pulled her sideways, gathering her against the warmth of his shoulder. "Where were you when I was younger?" she asked him. "When everyone called me Frizzy Tizzy? When I was falling in love with Cory? Why weren't you there?"

"I wish I had been," he answered her.

"Sugar, my heart is gone. I gave it to an inconsiderate jerk, and as wonderful as you are, I don't have anything left to give."

Sugar silenced her with a finger across her lips. "Cory's a lucky guy."

"Krystal's a lucky girl."

"What's that supposed to mean?"

Nance pulled back and looked up at him. "I'm

not Krystal Adkins' biggest fan. We may never be friends, but she does love you, Sugar. And you know what? I think Krystal is a forever girl, too. The other girl, the good-time girl—that's an act."

"Then how did I end up in her bed?"

"I don't know. Obviously, she took advantage of the situation. But, like you said, it's been two years, and you're still in her heart. Forgive her, Sugar. Forgive yourself and start over."

"Just like that?" Sugar's question had a cynical edge to it.

"Sure. This is pop psychology."

"Yeah, it is." Sugar put the SUV in reverse and made his way through the parking lot. His lack of response left Nance wondering whether she had offended him with her comments.

They didn't speak on the short drive back to the office. It wasn't until Sugar pulled up before Corance and they said their good-byes, with Nance thanking Sugar for lunch, that he finally answered her.

He gazed at Nance with clouded eyes, his blonde, twisted hair incongruent against the serious cast of his features. "It's not forgiveness, Nance," he said, his mouth twisted with bitterness. "It's trust. How can I trust a girl who seems like forever, but acts like a one-night stand?"

CHAPTER NINE

Two weeks. She'd been gone for two weeks, but already she felt out of place, or in this case, out of step. The Foot Fetish had become as alien to Krystal as Mars.

Oddly enough, she didn't miss the Fetish. Instead, she felt that the person she was before—the one who had worked at the Fetish—was a completely different person. The only thing that remained of her former self, was her love for Sugar Smith.

Somehow, in this new job at Corance, she'd found the path to becoming the person she was meant to be. With a jolt of insight, Krystal realized that she was truly happy at Corance.

She loved her new job. Her life seemed possessed of possibilities now. She'd never felt like this working at the Fetish. It didn't matter anymore that she'd taken the job to make Sugar jealous, Krystal wanted to stay at Corance and possibly even learn more about computers.

The fetish was her past.

Krystal searched the interior of the store, looking around with the eyes of a stranger, searching for the familiar, the comforting, the welcome that spoke of homecoming.

Instead, the Fetish was as it had always been. Garish, with splash-red signs selling false promises: Hot. Sexy. Babe.

And leather. The place reeked of leather. Berber carpet—mauve, flecked with pinks and purples—and the sales girls—bouffy-haired, Hooter wannabes wearing those awful maroon bolo-jackets with the high-heel logo.

One of them was coming toward her now, an uncertain smile on a smooth, brown face, chemically straightened hair teased to towering height and massed around a Kewpie-doll face.

"Tamara!" Krystal exclaimed, moving forward to give the girl a hug.

Tamara returned the embrace and then stepped back to study Krystal.

"Talk about moving on up." Tamara smiled, but the grin was still uncertain.

Krystal touched a self-conscious hand to her new hair-style. It was staid and boring by Fetish standards, but she liked it. The cut was sleekly professional, and it took her only a few moments to style, rather than the hour of teasing and spraying and combing.

She was wearing one of her new outfits, too: a taupe-colored skirt paired with a black thigh-length jacket. She'd picked it up on discount at the KASPAR store in the outlet mall on Hudson Street.

The shoes, a pair of no-nonsense black flats, had come from Hush Puppies, a store she hadn't known existed. The flats were so dull by fetish standards, they weren't even on the radar.

Tamara glanced down at Krystal's shoes, a habit ingrained in shoe store employees. It was still the first thing Krystal noticed about people. She didn't notice looks, or color, or oddities. She noticed shoes.

She could almost read Tamara's mind about the flats. Boring. Staid. Dull.

So what? Maybe her shoes were boring, but it didn't matter. The only thing that mattered was the look she'd seen in Sugar's eyes when he'd stopped in at Corance last week.

She was wearing her white flats then. Embarrassed by her conservative appearance, she'd waited for derision to appear on his features. It hadn't.

He actually seemed to like her better when she was dressed this way. He'd gone to lunch with Nance, of course, but it was the first time in years that Sugar had given her a compliment on her appearance. Best of all, he'd been sincere.

Would he be as interested today?

That was the real reason she'd stopped by, hoping to have an answer to that question.

Unfortunately, Sugar wasn't there. Tamara shooed the last of the part-time store clerks out the door and flipped over the cardboard 'open' sign to 'closed.'

"Where is he?" When Krystal worked at the fetish, she and Sugar always worked the closing shift together.

"You're not still hung up him, are you?" Tamara asked.

"I'm not hung up on him."

"What do you call it?"

"I call it love." With complete disregard for her tony outfit, Krystal pulled the sweeper from the store room and rolled it across the dusty floor carpet.

"Girl, you need to get a grip," Tamara told her as she counted out the money from the cash drawer. "Sugar has moved on."

Krystal stopped sweeping. "What do you mean?"

"I mean Sugar's not thinking about you. He's all up into computers. He's taking classes at the Globe, and I'm thinking it's because of that computer chick."

"Nance?" Krystal's expression was incredulous. "Nance Hadley?"

"That's the one."

Krystal rolled her eyes skyward, dismissing Nance with a shrug. "Girl, don't scare me like that. You really had me going for a minute. Nance Hadley's nothing. Have you seen her? She's not even cute."

Tamara snorted. "She might not be cute, but she's got Sugar's number. I'm telling you, Kris, it's time for you to move on." Her tone softened. "Look, I'm not trying to be a jerk. I'm not one of these Black women who gets upset when she sees our men crossing the color line, although I did have my eye on Sugar for a minute or two."

"Well, you have good taste, but the doggone man is mine," Krystal laughed. She returned the sweeper to the store room and then joined Tamara beside the register.

"That's the problem, Kris," Tamara pointed out. "The man don't know he's yours. I'm sick of seeing you put your heart on the line for Sugar. He's not interested. In fact, he's done everything he can to make sure you understand that."

"Sugar loves me. He just won't admit it."

"Has he told you he loves you?"

"No." Krystal hated the defensive note in her voice, but she couldn't help it. She was sick of having to defend herself. "He doesn't have to tell me."

"Okay…" Tamara drew the word out. "Can you say delusional?"

Krystal folded her arms over her chest. "No, I can't. And no, I'm not."

"From where I sit, you're headed for a rubber room and an oh-so-fashionable strait jacket."

"You're not funny." Krystal smiled in spite of herself.

"I'm beyond funny."

"Believe what you want." Krystal shrugged. She was used to people thinking she was off her rocker. After all, she'd been in love with Sugar forever. And maybe she was crazy, but she just knew that she and Sugar were meant to be together. The feeling came from the very depths of her heart. It was a part of her, and she would hold on to that belief until the day Sugar Smith married someone else.

"Sugar is just fighting his attraction to me," she said, keeping her tone light.

"For two years?" Tamara's gaze was incredulous.

"He's a great fighter?"

Tamara laughed and began switching off the lights. "You're the one with the sense of humor."

"Well, I can't believe Sugar is trying to hide behind Nance Hadley's skirt. As if!"

"As if, did you ever stop to think that maybe Sugar likes his chicks plain?"

"He loves me." Krystal knew she sounded like a warped CD stuck in the same spot. But he did love her. He just refused to realize it.

Tamara threw her hands up in defeat. "Whatever. I've tried. You keep chasing that boy until he ends up at the altar with somebody else. I'll be happy to sell you the shoes to wear to the wedding."

"You're a real encouragement."

"I call 'em like I see 'em."

"Sugar is mine. He always has been."

"Yeah? Well don't go trying to get harsh on me with your Sugar addiction."

"The first time I saw Sugar, I knew he was the guy for me. I don't care if I sound stupid, it's true."

"Grief, Krystal, you got to watch yourself. You're really starting to creep me out with that kind of talk. You keep talking crazy, then you'll be acting crazy. Don't think I won't give your narrow rear up to the police if you off that computer chick."

Krystal laughed. "I'm not offing anybody, least of all Nance Hadley." She stopped. "Then, again, maybe you're right, Tamara."

"What are you talking about?"

"Maybe old Frizzy needs a scare."

"You do not want to do that."

"Why not?"

"Because I was here that day she hired you. Frizzy, or whatever you want to call her, has that helpless-chick act down pat. Real-world Survival Rule One: Don't mess with the helpless-looking ones. They've been bullied so much, they start taking karate, carrying guns, calling the police when they see your crazy mug standing outside on the front step. Trust me on this one, Kris."

"Oh, yeah. Like old Frizzy could stand breaking a sweat. You don't know what it's like, Tamara. The woman's not helpless, she's perfect."

Krystal could see that Tamara wasn't persuaded. And, suddenly, it seemed important to convince her—or, was it herself whom she wanted to convince?

"I'm serious. The woman is... she's absolute perfection," she persisted, "From the top of her head to the soles of her feet. Every morning she comes floating into the office wearing these perfect outfits that cost a b'zillion dollars each. Everybody likes her. If I said one thing against her, you'd think I'd dissed the president, or something."

"Oh yeah?"

"Yeah. And she keeps that company running smoother than a free leg waxing."

"You almost sound like you like her."

"Right now, I'm her pet project. She's trying to make me over into this corporate Stepford wife."

"I missed that one."

"Oh, you know, perfect hair, perfect clothes, scandals kept in the basement."

"So, you don't buy the makeover thing?"

"Sure, I buy it. If your parents are rich. If you go to the right schools, meet the right people. Changing the outside doesn't change the inside. The rest of us are stuck like runt pigs at the feeding trough."

"I'm not country enough to get the joke, but if that's true, how come Sugar's going to computer school? He wants better than the Foot Fetish. In fact, I do, too. I'm thinking about going to school myself."

"You?" Krystal was nonplussed. "What would you do if you went to school?"

"I don't know."

"See," Krystal said triumphantly.

"Interior design," Tamara said suddenly. She dropped her eyes to the worn mauve carpet, awkward in the revelation of closely-held dreams. "I always wanted to do interior design."

"Really?" Krystal was surprised and then wondered why she should be. Tamara did have lots of style. The idea didn't seem so far-fetched after all.

"It's just, well, who would hire a black woman to decorate her home?"

"I don't know, Tamara." But someone would. Krystal suddenly felt as though everyone around her had boarded the bus and left her standing alone at the depot. They were all moving forward, and she was the only one fighting the momentum. But, giving up meant joining forces with Nance Hadley.

"I didn't think there was a chance for me to live my dreams either, until Nance Hadley hired you. Now you're waltzing in here, dressed to the nines in *absolute perfection*. You don't even look like the same person. And Sugar's off taking computer classes."

"He's not doing it because of Nance Hadley."

"Maybe not, but they'll have a lot in common. He's already been offered a job by a recruiting firm. He hasn't even finished taking his first week of class yet, and folks are circling him like he's a star athlete."

Tamara looked up, meeting Krystal's gaze with a challenging stare. "From where I sit, Nance Hadley's not the enemy."

Krystal didn't reply.

Maybe it was true that Nance Hadley only brought good things into their lives; but, if so, then why did Krystal feel so certain that Nance possessed the power to take from her the only thing she'd ever wanted in her life: the love of Sugar Smith?

CHAPTER TEN

Maybe Tamara was right. Maybe Krystal was certifiable. She was as loony as the state bird of Minnesota. In fact, they could do away with the loon as the state bird and stick Krystal Adkins' face on all those tourism posters.

"She's a home-town loon, don't'cha know," would serve just fine as the slogan.

After all, what reason, other than insanity, could she possibly give for hiding out in her car like some kind of crazed stalker, across the street from Nance Hadley's huge house.

Crazy.

And going to all the trouble of finding Nance's address, then not having the courage to go right up to the door and make her presence known. Krystal wasn't only crazy, she was also a coward. But it wasn't fear of Nance that immobilized Krystal. It was the sight of the cranberry SUV parked in Nance's circular driveway that stopped her cold.

What was Sugar doing at Nance's house?

The only possibility Krystal could think of was the one she didn't want to imagine. She closed her eyes, heart pounding as though she'd just run a mile, and blood rushing with the force of a turbulent river in her ears.

If she were as crazy as everyone thought her to be, she would get out of the car and march across the street. She pictured herself knocking on the door, confronting Nance, confronting Sugar.

She couldn't do it.

Sugar already believed the worst about her. He already believed she was easier than a batch of bake-and-serve cookies. And, coward that she was, she didn't have the courage to tell him that he was wrong. She didn't have the courage to tell him the truth.

Two years ago, she'd watched him from her car, much like she did now, her heart racing at the sight of him. For months, they worked in the same retail center, Krystal at a card shop four stores away from the Fetish. She'd kept hoping to bump into Sugar, to work up the courage to introduce herself, but Sugar always passed by without a second glance.

So she decided to get a job at the Fetish. At first, it seemed that she and Sugar clicked. He liked her. But he was a professional, so he kept a careful distance between himself and all the employees.

After a month of getting nowhere, Krystal made the decision to do whatever it took to get Sugar's attention. Maybe at the Christmas party, she thought. Maybe she could get his attention then.

She took extra care preparing for that party, her heart filled with both hope and a strange, anticipatory dread. If she couldn't get Sugar's attention that night, then she would forget about him. She would move on, she decided.

Krystal was one of the first to arrive at the party and was so terrified, she could barely respond to simple conversation. However, after several hastily swallowed cups of Christmas punch, she was feeling pretty good about things.

Then she saw Sugar. Her stomach had filled with a strange, fluttery feeling. Sugar was so handsome. She loved everything about him: his brown eyes that lit with a fire whenever he talked, his beautiful smile, his smooth, brown skin washed over a smooth, squared jaw. Most of all, she loved his blonde, twisted braids.

Although others looked in askance at the dark-rooted, blonde braids, Krystal knew why he chose the style. Beyond the fact that it suited him, she intuitively understood that Sugar Smith was a man who refused to be framed by his ethnicity.

He wasn't just a black man. He was Sugar Smith, a creative, intelligent, man. He was a man full of warmth and humor and nobility, and enough rebellion to hate being stereotyped.

It was that very quality that attracted Krystal the most.

It was that quality that had drawn her to him like a moth to a bright light.

In keeping with the celebratory atmosphere of the evening, Sugar was in an expansive mood. He'd also had several cups of the punch. Thinking back, Krystal wondered if it was the punch that had caused him to ask her to dance? She didn't want to believe that. Still, the only thing she knew for sure was that one dance led to another, and then another.

It was after the last dance that Krystal found herself leading an unresisting Sugar to her car. He made no protest as she drove to her apartment, and when she turned down the lights and switched on the music from a jazz CD, he'd been a willing participant in trading kisses and exploratory touches.

Nevertheless, planning a seduction and following through were two different things. Krystal had no experience in the real thing. Terrified, she led Sugar to her bedroom. There, losing her courage, she excused herself and hid in the bathroom until she could work up the courage to tell him that she wasn't a one-night-stand kind of girl.

She had fallen in love with Sugar on sight, but her love for him had grown as she'd come to know him. What she felt for Sugar was real and deep and precious. She couldn't bear to take advantage of the situation, grabbing at opportunity as if her affection were something cheap.

She wanted so much more from Sugar.

If she couldn't have the commitment, she didn't want to cheapen what she felt for him by turning it into a brief, physical encounter.

By the time she returned to her bedroom Sugar had passed out, or fallen asleep from the effects of the alcohol. Relief filled Krystal. Not considering how Sugar would interpret her actions, she removed his shoes and shirt, then she lay next to him, fantasizing that she and Sugar were married and that they slept together every night.

The next morning Krystal was up early. She showered, dressed, and prepared a huge breakfast for Sugar. She was in the middle of pouring coffee when he entered the room, his rumpled shirt hastily buttoned, his shoes on, and a frown on his face.

"Good morning, lover boy," Krystal chirped, making a joke of the situation.

Sugar wasn't amused. In clear, distinct words he told her that he did not sleep with employees. He apologized for taking advantage of her and said that it would not happen again.

Krystal tried to tell him that he hadn't taken advantage of her, but he refused to listen. He told her that he wouldn't bring up the subject again, and asked her to not speak about it as well, especially not to the other employees.

By that time, Krystal was furious. Of all the clod-headed things! Was he ashamed of her? He hadn't even given her a chance to explain!

Some sense of mischief prompted Krystal to put down the coffee pot and move seductively across the room to Sugar. She trailed a teasing finger from his cheek down to the top of his belly button. Draping an arm over his left shoulder she drawled, "Now, Sugar, why ever would I want to spoil our fun by telling everyone about it?"

A tic pulsed on the side of his cheek. Whether from anger or attraction, Krystal couldn't tell.

"There will be no repeat of last night," he told her.

It was attraction. Krystal realized. He likes me and he's struggling against it. The thought made her angrier than ever. She chucked Sugar on the chin, and with a daring she didn't know she possessed, pushed herself up on her tiptoes and planted a long and loving kiss on his firm lips.

She might have forgotten herself completely, but after a moment Sugar put her from him, his strong fingers wrapping around her arms with a gentleness that belied his aggressive expression.

"Sugar!" Krystal dropped the temptress act. "Come on, there's no reason to be upset." She started to tell him that nothing had happened between them, but something kept her from speaking the words.

Maybe it was that she could see that he was attracted to her. She could see that he was tempted by her.

Why was he holding back?

Was he just afraid?

Was it because of their racial differences? Surely not. Minneapolis was a liberal city where interracial relationships were as commonplace as traffic tickets. But, perhaps Sugar had reservations. Krystal had to prove to him that she loved him, that she could be worthy of him—despite their differences. She decided that from then on, she would be the woman who tempted Sugar.

From that point on, her clothing grew outrageous. She bought an entire line of teased-hair wigs, and she adopted a flippant tone with everyone around her. Now it seemed she had worn her adopted persona for so long that she couldn't remember the person she'd been. Or had she even existed before becoming the brash, flamboyant Krystal Adkins whom Sugar knew?

Over the last two weeks, she'd felt almost as if she were regaining bits and pieces of her true self, the person she'd given up to become the type of woman she thought Sugar would like.

And it was all for nothing.

Frizzy Tizzy, plain, old Nance Hadley, had snatched Sugar right from under Krystal's nose!

Tears gathered in Krystal's eyes and then, like a dam bursting, spilled over onto her cheeks. Racked by painful sobs, Krystal felt as though she was pouring out the last bit of her broken heart.

When someone rapped against the window of her car, she was so caught up in her grief, she didn't notice. It wasn't until the person knocked again, that a startled and mortified Krystal glanced over to see Frizzy Tizzy waving at her, a look of concern plastered across her plain face.

Hastily, Krystal scrubbed at the moisture on her cheeks. At a loss for the proper response, she rolled down the window and faced her rival.

"What do you want?" she snapped.

Nance stepped back and sighed. "I wanted to find out if you were okay."

"I'm fine," Krystal's reply was clipped.

"No, Krystal. You were crying."

"I had something in my eye."

Nance snorted. "Of all the lame...."

"What's Sugar doing here?" Krystal interrupted, her tone heavy with accusation.

Nance grew still. "In case you haven't noticed, Sugar is gone. And he was here, because he was invited." Her tone was reserved. "Why are you here?"

"It's a free country." The flippancy was delivered in a wavering voice and suddenly, Krystal couldn't keep pretending.

Her face crumpled.

A whimper turned into a sob. Then Krystal Adkins was blubbering like a four year old crying for a lost toy. And she was doing so in front of Nance Hadley, her worst enemy in the world.

CHAPTER ELEVEN

"Come on." Nance pulled the car door open and, grabbing hold of Krystal's arm, hauled her from the car.

"I.... No! Let go of me!" Krystal struggled, but Frizzy had a power-grip hold. Nance was able to get her out of the car, then she kicked the door shut with her foot. Krystal was reminded of Tamara's comment regarding the helpless types.

Heedless of Krystal's protests, Nance pulled her across the street, telling her, "Scream all you want. My neighbors are used to my assaulting people."

In spite of herself, Krystal smiled, but she refused, absolutely refused to warm up to Nance Hadley.

Nance propelled Krystal through a double glass door entry into a two-story foyer tiled in flagstone.

"Wow." Momentarily startled by the elegant grandeur of Nance's home, Krystal stopped struggling, her eyes roving over the wrought iron, double stairway that curved in an arch over a sun-bathed hearth room with floor-to-ceiling transom windows overlooking a stone terrace and pool.

"Wow," Krystal repeated.

"Yeah, yeah, welcome." Nance tugged on Krystal's arm. "I'll give you the tour later, providing you behave yourself."

"Maybe I don't want a tour," Krystal responded tartly, but she allowed Nance to tow her through a spacious hallway and into the kitchen.

"Sit," Nance commanded and pushed Krystal onto a tall chair before the center island.

"Why are you doing this?" Krystal was suddenly exhausted, worn out by fear and sorrow. "Look, I wasn't doing anything wrong. I mean, I just wanted to talk, and then I saw Sugar's car...." she trailed off, her heart so filled with anguish, she wasn't sure if she wouldn't start crying again.

Nance didn't respond. Instead, she busied herself filling a tea kettle with cold water and turning up the heat beneath it on the stove. She took delicate china cups from the cabinet and placed one on the kitchen island in front of Krystal, and the other on the counter beside her. She added a sugar bowl filled with artificial sweetener, a small pitcher of cream, and a squeeze bottle of lemon juice.

"What are you doing?" Krystal asked after a moment.

"What does it look like I'm doing?"

"You're making tea?"

"Bingo," Nance answered.

"Why?"

"It's the equivalent of boiling hot water when someone is having a baby."

"Okay."

Nance met Krystal's stare. "Look Krystal, I'm not interested in feuding with you, but you want a fight. In fact, you've wanted a fight since the first day we met. Well, I'm tired of trying to be a peacemaker. If you want a fight, you've got it, but we're going to do this the civilized way."

"Over tea?" Krystal's expression was disbelieving.

"Over tea, and I think I have some cucumber sandwiches from my last over-tea fight."

"Funny." Who knew Frizzy had a sense of humor?

"Don't do cucumber sandwiches? We'll do cookies then." Nance withdrew a tin of Chelsea walnut cookies from the pantry, and continued speaking, her tone conversational. "I think I've finally got you figured out Krystal."

"Oh, really?" Krystal tried an unconcerned slouch over the tea cup, but it was too uncomfortable trying to lounge in the sheath dress. She straightened.

Nance placed the cookies on a plate and stuck them in front of Krystal. "I think so."

"What's your take, Frizella?" Krystal took one of the cookies and nibbled at the edge. It gave her something to do with her hands.

"That's one for no tour, Krystal."

"You're counting me out like I'm a little kid?" Krystal was nonplussed.

"You behave like a rebellious teenager, so I'll treat you like one. We're not that far apart in age. I also know you're not the bad girl you want everyone to think you are. I expect you to drop the act. Otherwise, it's not a fair fight."

"What makes you think I fight fair?"

"Because, you're no different from me."

It was a relief to give up the battle to flash attitude. "Now that's where you wrong, Miss High-and-Mighty Nance Hadley. You and I, we're nothing alike." She spread her hand in a sweeping gesture. "Look at this set-up. You have everything you want. And, it doesn't matter how hard I try...." The tears were starting again. "Nothing ever works out for me...."

Krystal hopped down from the stool. Feeling like the biggest idiot in the world, she clasped her hands together, saying, "I've already made a fool out of myself, so I guess it doesn't matter what you think of me, but I'm willing to beg."

More craziness. More absolute lunacy, but when had Krystal Adkins done anything in half-measures? She wouldn't start now, not when it was so important to her. She'd been pushed beyond the limits of her endurance.

Nothing mattered anymore.

Desperate beyond reason, she hiked the sheath up a couple of inches and got down on her knees before Nance Hadley, her head bowed in humiliation and shame and need.

"Please, Nance." She looked up with pleading eyes. "Please, let me have Sugar. You don't love him like I do. I'll do anything you ask. Anything."

Amazement and wonder battled with compassion on Nance's features. And then, surprisingly, a tear slipped into a sad, downward path on her cheek. Disregarding the expensive chiffon dress she wore, Nance joined Krystal on the floor. She reached out and gave Krystal an awkward embrace. "You're a kernel shy of a full ear of corn, you know?"

Embarrassed by this unexpected accord, Krystal felt compelled to respond to the hug with a hesitant pat on Nance's back.

Frizzy Tizzy made disliking her next to impossible.

"It's my generation," Krystal replied as Nance pulled back. "We're extreme. But I'm not kidding about Sugar. I love him enough to do just about anything."

"Short of murder, I hope."

Krystal's answering smile held a trace of bitterness. "Morality is such a pain sometimes, but yes, short of murder."

"That's a relief."

"For you, maybe." Krystal closed her eyes. "For me, it's torture. I'm stuck. I can't think of anything but Sugar. And you. Together."

Nance's answer was interrupted by the shrill whistle of the tea kettle, the loud noise startled them both. Nance lifted herself from the floor and then turned back to pull Krystal up as well.

Taking the kettle from the heat, she poured hot water into both cups. "I don't have any loose tea, but I've got a good variety of bagged tea. English breakfast, apricot, green, peach, strawberry-kiwi, and Darjeeling. I've even got some chai if you're in a funky mood."

Funky fit. "Give me the chai." Krystal climbed back onto the barstool.

Nance handed her a packet of peach chai and sat down across from her at the island. Meeting Krystal's stare, Nance said, "Sugar and I are not together."

Hope flared in Krystal's chest. "Then why was he here?"

Nance stirred her spoon around in her cup. "You know Sugar's taking computer courses?"

"I heard something to that effect."

"Sugar's a real go-getter. He's taking a JAVA course, and he's already read the entire course book—in one week. Now he's working on learning *XML*. That type of initiative is rare. I want him working for Corance. We're working on some I2 projects."

"I2?"

"Internet 2. Not enough bandwidth on the current internet, so the powers-that-be are developing a second internet. That's the one that will replace TV, no doubt, but who knows. And programmers with the kind of initiative Sugar has, well, I offered him a job."

"Really!" Krystal's eyes shone with excitement. "He's going to love working at Corance."

"He's a good fit for the type of employee we want. He shows initiative. He's open-minded, an explorer. In any case, the important thing is that you understand that Sugar and I were talking business."

"Why here?" Krystal couldn't resist asking. "Why not meet at a coffee bar, or something?"

"Sugar's my friend. Not that it matters, but I was on my way home when he called to thank me for encouraging him to take a computer course." Nance's gaze was direct. "His teacher at Globe College had already introduced him to some top companies, and he felt that I'd played a part in his success."

"But you didn't."

"No," Nance agreed. "I told him that. He made his own opportunities—with others, and with Corance. I asked him to meet me here to learn more. I really like Sugar. He's smart. He's wise and wonderful, but there's nothing romantic going on between us."

"How much longer will that last?" Krystal asked bitterly.

Nance took a moment to answer. "I won't lie. I wish I could be attracted to Sugar. I admire him. I like him a lot, but the spark isn't there. I don't think it ever will be."

Krystal sipped at the chai. "Because you're in love with Cory?"

Nance's expression closed off. Krystal could see it. "My feelings for Cory are...."

"Private?" Krystal interrupted with a lifting of her eyebrows. "If that's the case then all that getting down on your knees with me was just patronizing."

"I wasn't trying to be patronizing."

"Then be honest. You can see every piece of dirty linen I own. I want to see your dirty drawers, Frizzy. I want to know why you don't want Sugar. Is it because you could never love anyone but Cory? Or, are you going to change your mind next week?"

Nance hopped down from the barstool and made an unnecessary trip to the refrigerator. She returned with a jar of pickles which she sat on the table with a thump.

"Okay." She opened the jar. "Okay. Everyone knows how I feel...used to feel...about Cory. I mean, it's like I wore a neon sign with the words '*Cory's fool*' plastered on my forehead. But, that's in the past."

"Why? Because of me? Did I break you up?"

Nance shrugged.

"If it's because of me, then from what I've seen, Cory's over his nine-day infatuation. He never really wanted me in the first place. For some reason, he just wanted a trophy chick to flash around."

Nance sat down hard on her chair, dropping the lid to the pickle jar onto the counter. "Exactly." Her eyes were bright with unshed tears. "Cory wants a trophy wife—someone young and beautiful, with perfect features. He wants someone like you."

Krystal's smile was big with relief. "You know, for someone so smart, you can be pretty dumb at times, Frizzy."

"Thank you. I'm well aware of my shortcomings."

"No, listen. Don't get your Victoria Secrets in a wad. All I'm saying is that looks are just like anything else—you can buy them."

"Why does everyone keep saying that? I'm not having plastic surgery on the off-chance that Cory might fall in love with me if I got a new nose."

"Whose talking plastic surgery? I'm talking about working with what you have, but I don't think you want that either."

"What's that supposed to mean?"

"I've realized something about you, too. You're afraid of being beautiful. You'd rather compete based on your brains than on your looks."

"I wonder why?"

"Well, it's not because you're ugly."

"I'm so cute I've got men falling over themselves to ask me out."

"You've got my man asking you out."

"The only reason Sugar was interested in me was because I was an anomaly. No offense, but he's pushing shoes for a living, and yet, he's bright and full of curiosity. He's bored. I was a change from the normal BARB customer."

"What's a BARB?"

Nance opened her mouth to explain and then thought better of it. The expression was demeaning. Not just to the women to which she'd applied it, but to herself. BARBS had their problems, Nance had hers. And while Nance couldn't find much value in an attitude of focusing on physical attributes rather than personal capabilities, BARB was a word she would never again use. "Never mind," she told Krystal. "It's just that I was different. Like a puzzle he wanted to figure out."

"And has he?"

"Figured me out?" Nance's smile seemed a

shade too mysterious to Krystal. "What's to figure out? I'm an open book. What Sugar and I have begun is a good friendship."

"And Cory?"

"Past."

The way she said the word sent a chill through Krystal. Maybe she wasn't as brainy as Frizzy, but she was smart enough to know that some of the best romantic relationships started as friendships. Even if Nance didn't think she wanted Sugar now, she might change her mind in the future.

"You know, Nance, I hear Cory is the one doing the chasing these days."

"Chasing what?"

"You."

"Until someone better comes along." Nance's voice was flat.

"I don't think you ever gave yourself a chance with Cory. Even if he is in your past, you should at least use him to practice attracting your future."

"What?"

"You ever watch those talk shows where they do the makeovers?"

Nance stiffened. She looked about as huffy as a teen-aged girl who'd been stood up on prom night. In a sharp, irritated tone she replied, "Putting lipstick on and combing my hair in a pouf is not going to make me beautiful."

"You'd be surprised," Krystal kept her tone light. "Men tend to be visual."

"Meaning?"

"Take Cory, for instance. The boy barely got my name. His eyes were roving over me like I was a porterhouse steak and him a starving man."

"Spare me the gory details," Nance said. "Besides, you're just proving my point. I can't compete based on looks. I'd have to smear lipstick over my entire face just to get Cory's attention, and then I'd be lucky to get anything beyond a laugh and a pointing finger."

She took her empty cup to the sink and rinsed it out. "I practically begged Cory to marry me," she spoke quietly, her back to Krystal. "It was humiliating. There's no way I'm going to set myself up so that Cory can step on my heart again."

Like a tangible force, waves of pain seemed to ripple from Nance. Or maybe it was just that Krystal understood exactly what she was going through.

Perhaps Nance was right. Maybe they weren't so different after all.

"I've done the same thing with Sugar," Krystal told her.

Nance turned. "We make a pretty sight, don't we? Sitting here, moaning about man trouble. Elsie would not be pleased with us."

"Yeah," Krystal agreed and gave Nance a watery smile. "I hate complaining anyway. It seems like such a useless activity. It doesn't ever change anything."

"I know."

"Look, Nance, I have an idea. You might think it's stupid, but I've already made a big fool of myself, so I figure it won't hurt."

"What's your idea?"

"A makeover."

"I told you, I don't want a makeover."

"Not just you. I'm talking a makeover for me too." Krystal drained the last of the chai and rose to place her cup in the sink. "I can recommend a great hairstylist. I can give you a few tips on makeup technique. You do the same for me."

You're kidding."

"Nope. I'm as serious as a pimple on prom night."

"Ugh," Nance grimaced, and then asked, "What's the purpose?"

"The purpose is simple, Frizzy. You and I are going to show those men of ours not to judge a book by its cover. We're going to teach them a lesson they'll never forget. When they're done apologizing for being cluckers, then we'll forgive them and live happily ever after. Now, are you in, or not?" Krystal waited expectantly.

Nance had the appearance of someone who wanted something so much that she could taste it.

But would she do it?

At last, a slow smile spread across Nance Hadley's plain face. The smile transformed her, lighting a spark of mischief in her pale-green eyes, making her almost beautiful. Krystal blinked and the moment passed.

"I'm in," Nance said. She stuck her hand out, clasping Krystal's in a firm shake.

"Good." Krystal returned the smile, a feeling of camaraderie welling inside her. They were honor-bound now, no longer enemies, but partners in purpose.

"Good," she repeated, a martial light appearing in her eye. "Trust me, Frizzy. After we're done, those boys won't know what hit 'em."

CHAPTER TWELVE

Saturday morning, four days after she had agreed to the makeover pact, a reluctant Nance met Krystal at Spalon Montage in Woodbury's Tamarack Shopping Center.

Their agreement had the effect of forcing Krystal and Nance into an uneasy friendship. As a consequence, things were much more pleasant around the office. Even so, as Nance waited in the foyer of the salon before the half-circle reception desk, she couldn't help but wish that she hadn't agreed to the makeover.

It just felt like so much ado over nothing. The last thing Nance wanted was to get her hopes up and then come away with nothing more than a brand new hairstyle.

Besides, even if the makeover were successful and she was suddenly the most beautiful woman in the world, it wouldn't solve her problems with Cory—problems that seemed to have grown worse than ever.

To be honest, much of the existing tension between her and Cory was a result of her own behavior. Wisely, in Nance's opinion, Cory had said nothing about Nance's lunch date with Sugar.

Instead, he'd continued sending her flowers. But how could she accept the gifts when she felt as though they were bribes? Cory was just trying to cajole her into forgiving him. Refusing to give in to his charm, Nance had responded by giving every one of the bouquets to Krystal. After seeing the flowers show up on Krystal's desk for two days straight, Cory stopped sending them.

Since then, he'd maintained an injured silence whenever Nance was around. Conversation between the two of them was stilted and unnatural, centering mainly upon business topics.

Nance was miserable, but she refused to show it. Instead, she laughed and joked her way through the day, treating Cory with a brisk, off-hand joviality that only seemed to intensify his irritability.

Nance consoled herself with the knowledge that misery was part of getting over a bad love affair. She'd loved Cory Miller for most of her life; she'd have been a fool to expect to walk away from a lifetime of caring and not feel pain. She'd be a bigger fool if she expected a makeover to change things between them.

Krystal's rushed arrival brought Nance out of her dismal thoughts. The two women greeted each other with a wary friendliness, and then Krystal led Nance to the reception desk to check in before moving over to the wait area.

"We'll do a trade," Krystal suggested as they flipped through magazines highlighting different hair styles. "You choose my style, I choose yours."

Although Krystal no longer wore her hair in the mile-high teases she'd sported on their first meeting, Nance wasn't certain about the wisdom of allowing the former BARB to select anything for her, least of all something as long-lived as a bad hairstyle. But Krystal, seeing the hesitancy in Nance's eyes said, "Hey, Frizzy, I'm in the same boat. I have to trust you, you have to trust me. If you don't like the style I pick, you can pay me back by choosing something equally scary. Besides, Michelle's reputation is at stake. She's not going to butcher your hair so that I can fulfill some petty vendetta."

"Fine," Nance agreed reluctantly. Leaving Krystal in the waiting area, she followed Michelle to the shampoo station.

Thirty minutes later, she gazed at her reflection in the mirror with amazement. Her fears, she

A LIFETIME LOVING YOU 229

saw now, had been completely unwarranted. Krystal's choice of a completely radical, super-short cut was perfect.

The cut was boyish, tapering at the neck, with moussed spikes fingered into disarray on top. It was absolute perfection on Nance; better than plastic surgery because losing the ton and a half of hair revealed a delicately boned, heart-shaped face.

No frizzy fly-aways meant that sea-green eyes and full lips were the focus of attention, and the bright, striated, maple-leaf colors were warmed up and toned down to deep auburn with a henna Clay-Pac.

For years, Nance had moved through her life weighted by frizzy, unwieldy hair. Now, seeing the difference one simple little hair cut made, she felt all the more foolish for so strongly resisting the whole makeover idea.

If she'd had any clue of the difference, she'd have clipped her wild mane ages ago. She tossed her head, feeling the waves bounce around on her head, light and airy. She felt so free—a different person altogether.

"For pity's sake, Nance Hadley, you're better looking than Julia Roberts!" Krystal exclaimed when Michelle brought her over to view the results.

"Julia Roberts as Tinker Bell, or Julia Roberts as Julia Roberts?" Nance lifted a self-conscious hand to her newly cropped hair. Her cheeks burned with embarrassment as Krystal paced a circle around her, studying the cut with a critical eye.

"Forget Julia." Krystal waved her hand in a dismissive gesture. "This is your movie, baby. I know Michelle is good, but dang, Robin should give the girl her own salon." Krystal's smile was wide with satisfaction. She turned to the stylist and gave her a thumbs-up signal.

"I had no idea a hair cut could make so much difference," Nance admitted. It was difficult to stop staring, difficult to believe that the pixie face reflected in the mirror belonged to her.

Funny that she'd never noticed the sculpted cheekbones, or the full, inviting lips.

Had her mane of frizzy hair hidden them from her?

And her eyes, they were so large, she almost looked as *BARBish* as Krystal. It was her lips, she decided. The top lip was slightly larger than the bottom, giving her a pouty, come-hither look.

She sucked her lip in, but decided she looked silly. There was no help for it. It was something she couldn't change, and in all truth, the upper lip thing was cute in a quirky kind of way.

Nance hopped down from the stylist's chair and flashed Krystal a grateful smile.

"Don't smile at me," Krystal said, sounding as though she were half-serious, "I think I hate you."

Nance laughed. "That's too bad, because you've suddenly become my favorite person in the world."

"So you like it?" Krystal seemed anxious about Nance's response.

Nance nodded. "I love it, Krystal. I absolutely love it." She shook the curls one final time. "Now it's your turn."

"Yeah." Krystal suddenly looked uncomfortable. "Look, Frizzy…." She glanced at Nance's short style. "Guess I'll have to call you something different now."

"Buzz?" Nance offered with a smile.

"Nah, you're too much of a cream puff for that one. I'll come up with something, don't you worry. Anyway, I, well, the thing is…. Aw, I guess I might as well just show you." Krystal reached up and tugged at her page boy. It slipped off to reveal a thatch of jet black hair cut as short and boyish as Nance's new style.

Nance stared, her mouth wide open in shock. Krystal laughed, a weak sound that clearly revealed her discomfiture. "It's never grown beyond shoulder length." She couldn't quite meet Nance's gaze. "The girls who come in the Fetish..." her voice faded away. Then, taking a deep breath, she said. "Stupid. I know. It's just that I thought Sugar might notice me if I had long hair."

"But you said Michelle styles your hair." Nance was still reeling from shock.

"She styles my wigs when they start going flat."

"Does Sugar know it's a wig?"

"No. I bought it before. I knew I wanted to work at the Fetish, so I decided to rev up my look before interviewing there. I did a little market research, studying the customers and the employees—the Fetish tends to hire a certain look."

"Big hair, big boobs, I noticed."

"Yeah. That's us."

"I'm sorry, Krystal." Nance realized how judgmental she sounded. She'd made a vow not to think in those terms, not to judge others on such a shallow scale.

Krystal waved away the apology. "No. You're right, Nance. That's the Fetish look. And I understand, finally, that I've got more than physical attractiveness going for me. Anyway, before achieving this magnificient stage of enlightenment, I cut my hair short and started wearing a wig."

Nance thought of all the things she could say. A million things went through her mind, some of them guaranteed to make Krystal feel foolish, but she couldn't bring herself to speak words that might crush the girl's spirit. As ludicrous as her actions seemed, Krystal had done no less than Nance herself had. They'd both negated themselves to win love, yet, neither had gotten what she wanted.

Nance had misjudged Krystal, repeatedly, setting herself above the girl and believing that because she was a corporate executive in a large software company, she was somehow a more valuable person than Krystal.

Chagrined at the revelation, Nance reached out and laid a comforting hand on Krystal's slumped shoulder. "Who am I, Krystal? I know more about computers than I ever really wanted to know, because I thought it would help me attract Cory."

Krystal's responding smile was a light, brightening her features and highlighting her face. Seeing it, Nance was struck once more by Krystal's very obvious beauty.

Granted, Krystal was abrasive. She was a shade too forthright and supremely ill-mannered, but beneath the flaws there was a heart that beat with warmth and kindness and intelligence.

Krystal Adkins was one of those people who gave without expecting anything in return, and whose greatest strength was unending loyalty—once Krystal was a friend, she would always be a friend, no matter what.

Somehow they had to get Sugar to see the treasure in Krystal—something he'd never notice as long as he was confronted with gigantic hair and two tons of makeup.

In her own dealings with him, Nance had found Sugar to be a cut-to-the-chase kind of guy. He wouldn't fall for the person Krystal was pretending to be, not like Cory had. Nance ignored the twinge of bitterness. Cory was in the past.

With effort, she focused her complete attention on Krystal, saying, "Since I get to choose your hair style, I say, nix the wig. Go natural. Michelle can style your hair. We'll be twins."

Expression still hesitant, Krystal nodded and allowed Michelle to lead her to the shampoo chair. A short time later, Michelle beckoned Nance over to view her handiwork. "You guys almost look like sisters," she said as she sprayed a final gloss coating over Krystal's hair.

The two women stood side by side before the large mirror and gazed at their reflections. They were both petite, and slim, with delicate features. Although one was brunette with blue eyes, and the other auburn haired with green eyes, Michelle was right. They could have been related.

A look of comprehension passed between them.

"You don't think…" Nance started, and then stopped. The idea was too preposterous.

Krystal, however, had no compunction about speaking what was on her mind. "The guys saw the resemblance and chose whichever look was more comfortable for them?" She finished Nance's sentence.

Nance shrugged. The idea was too fantastic. She couldn't credit it. "It will be interesting to see their reactions," she said, and let the matter drop.

They verified an appointment for a makeup session later that evening, and then left the salon. Next on their list was shopping. They took Nance's car, leaving Krystal's little gas-saver Tercel at the salon. Krystal tried to coax Nance into leaving the top down on DB7, but Nance refused, afraid that she might destroy the magic of her new hairstyle. Cory might be in the past, but Nance wanted him to see her looking her best.

Before heading over to the outlet mall, they decided to stop in at Sunsets for lunch.

As she and Krystal waited for the server to bring their iced teas, Nance was struck by the oddity of the situation. Two weeks earlier, if anyone had said that she and Krystal would be sitting in Sunsets sharing a meal together in the best of spirits, she wouldn't have believed it.

But, there they were. And the conversation, rather than being stilted and uncomfortable, was, for the most part, lighthearted.

Krystal was not the enemy, Nance realized. In fact, at some point that morning Krystal Adkins had become a potential friend. Released from wrongly formed opinions regarding the younger woman, Nance found that she genuinely liked Krystal.

They didn't have a whole lot in common, although both had grown up in St. Paul.

Krystal's parents had divorced when she was five and she lived with her mother. Nance, on the other hand, was raised in a loving family with both parents working hard to nurture their only child.

Krystal moved to Woodbury after her mother accepted a job at one of the local insurance companies. Far from being a *hootchie*, Krystal hadn't even moved in to her own place until she was twenty-five, nor had she been on a date since meeting Sugar.

And while Nance had attended the University of Minnesota, earning an undergraduate degree in computer science and a master's degree in business administration, Krystal hadn't gone to college at all, although she'd won a scholarship. The scholarship had only covered a single year. According to Krystal, she turned it down knowing she couldn't afford to pay for the remaining three years. She'd worked at various places before the Fetish, including working a year at a card shop in the same strip mall. A couple of months after Sugar became the manager of the Fetish, she'd applied for a job at the shoe store.

Lunch went by quickly. They'd finished their meals and were waiting for the check when Nance, struck by sudden curiosity, asked Krystal, "When did you first realize that you were in love with Sugar?"

A funny look appeared on Krystal's face. Discomfort? Self-consciousness? Nance couldn't say for sure. Krystal just shrugged, her voice quiet as she said, "Before."

"Before?" Nance questioned, not understanding.

Krystal nodded, and seemed relieved when the waitress returned with their checks. "Before."

It was all she would say on the matter. Rather than press for clarification, Nance let it drop, but after thinking about it for a moment, she found that the answer actually made sense.

Krystal said "before," and Nance understood, because that's when she'd grown to love Cory. Before she'd even shown up on Cory's radar screen, Nance Hadley loved him. Before she'd become the person she was now, shaped and molded by the desire for Cory's esteem. Before she'd given up what she could have been to become what she thought he needed.

Now, as Nance sat in companionable silence with a woman who once had been her enemy, she wondered if any makeover, if any change of heart, if anything in the world could return to her the innocence she'd lost over the past two weeks.

Could anything possibly return her and Cory to "before"?

CHAPTER THIRTEEN

They entered the bowling alley, striding side by side. The brunette was dressed simply, a pair of jeans and a white T-shirt beneath an oatmeal-colored, V-neck cable sweater. Her make-up was applied with a feather touch: sparkling eyes, a light coat of mascara on lashes that were thick and long over misted gray eyes, the cheek bones were tinged a faint peach from excitement, not makeup. Her full lips were neutral except for the barely there gloss.

The other woman, the auburn-haired beauty, was more sophisticated. She wore tan form-fitting suede pants under a black thigh-length jacket and black boots. Her sea-foam eyes were large and luminescent, surrounded by thick brown lashes. Her skin was perfect, porcelain clear. Her lips were touched with a deep wine color that drew attention to their pouty quality. She was the more beautiful of the two, maybe because she carried herself with an unconscious grace and a dignity that spoke of more than just skin-deep beauty, while the brunette seemed to have just a shade of uncertainty.

The two women moved forward in tandem, ignoring the looks of appreciation, the rude whistles and calls from guys out with their buddies and looking for a good time. A couple of men even approached them as they stood waiting for the rental shoes, but those who tried making a connection received a charming brush-off for their trouble.

It was probable that most of the single guys in the Retro Bowl noticed Nance Hadley's and Krystal Adkins' entry.

Cory and Sugar didn't.

Sugar, seated at the scoring table across from Cory, who was perched on the side bench, was intent on explaining some principle of delivering three-dimensional content via entertainment webs to Cory.

Nance knew she shouldn't be nervous about Cory's perception of her appearance. After all, she'd washed her hands of him. She'd given him up, and tonight was nothing more than good friends out to have fun.

Nevertheless, it was disconcerting to be completely ignored. Anticipation gave way to irritation as the two girls stood to one side waiting to be noticed. Finally, a burst of anger propelled Nance over to Cory. He glanced up, startled, as she hooked her boot on the edge of the bench.

"Are we bowling tonight, or are you and Sugar planning to talk business all evening long?"

Cory stared up at her, a blank perplexity on his handsome face. After a moment, recognition dawned, and the perplexed expression transformed into amazement.

"Nance?" he asked cautiously.

A feeling of pleasure spread through Nance. Maybe the makeover hadn't been such a waste of time. But no. That kind of thinking was dangerous.

"If you're gonna' talk business," she continued, marveling at the brazenness of her tone, "then there are a couple of guys across the room over there who promised to show Krystal and me a roaring good time."

Cory opened his mouth, but nothing came out. With a tantalizing smile, Nance leaned forward and with a gentle chuck, pushed his mouth closed.

"There, don't want you catching flies. We're supposed to be bowling, not fishing." She straightened and, without waiting for his reply, faced

Sugar.

"Hey, Sugar."

"Nance," Sugar gave her a brief welcoming glance, but he appeared as stunned as Cory by their transformation. He took in Nance's appearance without comment before his gaze strayed back to Krystal. Everyone seemed frozen in some kind of visual time warp. The two men passing gazes from each other and then back to the women.

After several moments of silence, Nance took over, saying the thing that was on everyone's mind. "Krystal and I spent the day at Montage."

"You both look wonderful," Sugar said, his sincerity evident.

"You think so, Sugar?" Delight dawned in Krystal's eyes. "Because, this is my real hair and.... What I mean is, well...."

Sugar didn't let her finish. "That other stuff was a wig?" He was clearly surprised.

Krystal nodded. Her expression turned miserable. She turned a beseeching gaze to Nance.

"Yeah, it was time to dump the Fetish look," Nance caught the appeal and dove in, saying the first thing that came to mind. "Krystal's moving on with her life. Just like you, she has a great career ahead of her at Corance. We're thinking she might do something in marketing or product development."

"We are?" Cory asked.

"We are," Nance asserted. She was in the stratosphere now, winging it with all her might, but Krystal followed her lead without demur. There was a sense of trust between them.

"Absolutely," Krystal's smile was bright. "I love working at Corance. In fact, Nance has almost convinced me to go back to school."

"Really?" Sugar seemed doubtful. "What would you study? If you decide to go, that is?" he asked.

Krystal must have recognized his skepticism. Her reply was delivered in a tart voice. "I hear St. Thomas has some great programs for marketing. I'm not getting any younger, it's time I stopped waiting around for the sky, and started climbing the ladder up."

"Krystal's a woman with a great deal of promise," Nance interjected quickly. The last thing she wanted was for Krystal to set herself up with talk of how long she'd waited for Sugar to return her love. "We spent the entire day together," she added, secretly enjoying the twin expressions of shock that appeared on the men's faces. "After talking things through, we realized that we'd behaved horribly with the both of you."

"Right," Krystal agreed, although she sounded more confident than she appeared. The glance she turned toward Nance was definitely questioning.

"I, for one, am extremely embarrassed," Nance continued, hoping Krystal's cooperation would last. "We've done nothing but waste time fighting each other—trying to force you poor guys to return attraction, when clearly you're happier just being our friends."

"You going somewhere with this, Boo?" Cradling his head in his hands, Cory stretched out a pair of long, jeans-clad legs and stared at Nance, a hint of amusement lurking in his blue eyes.

"Well certainly," Nance return his gaze with a haughty stare. It was just like Cory Miller to take everything so lightly. It was a trait that had always irritated her. He was forever finding a silver lining in things.

Making a great show of ignoring Cory, Nance turned an encouraging glance to Krystal. The comments weren't something she'd rehearsed, but she was certain that as long as it seemed as though Krystal was chasing him, Sugar would continue to run. Sugar Smith was, at heart, a romantic hero. He wanted a woman he had to win.

"There's no need for us to put out lures like

you're prize trout on opening day," she continued.

Krystal frowned a bit, but nodded in agreement.

"Besides," Nance waved at a group of guys who were motioning for her and Krystal to come join them, "Why beat a dead horse?"

Cory glanced in the direction of Nance's wave. His grin faded, but he said nothing.

"Nance is right," Krystal chirped, her smile firmly in place as she wiggled her fingers at the wildly gesturing group of men. "So, there's no need for you guys to worry about saying the wrong thing. We're not looking to you for commitment. We're here for one thing."

"Bowling!" the two women finished together.

Krystal hooked her thumbs through the belt loops of her jeans. "So, are you guys ready to bowl, or what?"

With a sudden energy, Cory bounced from his seat and surprised them all by saying, "Nance is on my team," before anyone else could speak.

A traitorous thrill raced through Nance leaving her to wonder when, if ever, she would break free from the annoying wayward emotions.

Sugar glanced at Krystal as though seeking her confirmation.

"Fine by me," Krystal said with an admirable display of indifference.

As they waited to start the first set, Nance tried to read Cory, tried to see behind those devastating blue eyes of his to what he was thinking.

Had it been just four days since he'd kissed her? It seemed as though they'd been at odds with each other forever.

Nance couldn't recall ever having an argument with Cory that had lasted such a long time. Usually they were ready to end any tension between them within moments of a disagreement.

"How have you been?" she asked, and realized that it was the first time she'd ever had to ask the question. She'd always known how he was. She knew his schedule, knew whether he was happy or sad, his goals, his dreams, at least, she had. In just four short days, the separation between them had grown into a gulf that seemed almost impossible to bridge.

"You don't want an answer to that question, do ya', Boo?" Cory's tone was distant, as if they were strangers.

Nance pretended she didn't hear the comment. Adopting a brisk, business tone to match his, she said, "Development's ramping up to market version five of Web Mate. How's version six coming?"

"Nothing but bugs," Cory's smile was the first natural one he'd shown her in days. He pushed himself from the bench.

Lightly, he took a lock of her hair between two fingers. "I like your hair, Boo."

Nance blushed and called herself a fool. Some primordial force of nature swept her eyes downward like a demure teeny-bopper on a first date.

Grow up, she told herself. Making herself meet his gaze, she smiled and said, "Thanks."

Instead of releasing her hair as she'd expected, he moved even closer to her, until they were inches apart. "You're the most beautiful woman in the room." The whispered words sent shivers along her skin. She felt them, little goose bumps of pleasure raising along her arms. It took every ounce of will-power she possessed to resist the appeal in his blue eyes.

If only he'd said those words a month ago, or even two weeks ago. Then, the same statement would have sent her into a state of mindless euphoria.

Now, the words only served to highlight the problem between them.

Appearances.

His attraction to her was based on appearances.

Not that it was wrong to be attracted to a person's looks. Heaven knew Nance thought Cory Miller was the most handsome man to step a foot on God's green earth, but, in her heart of hearts, she knew that if he was in love with her because of her appearance, then she'd never feel secure.

She didn't want to live with the fear that the moment someone better looking came along, she might lose him. She couldn't bear it.

Sorrow settled against her heart like a dead weight, stiffening her into immobility. A brittle smile set her lips into a frozen grimace. "That's quite a compliment coming from someone as attractive as you," she quipped on a note of false cheeriness.

"Nance..." he said, and she could hear pain in his voice.

She hardened her heart. This whole fiasco was his fault. Not hers. He was the one who'd destroyed their friendship. He'd destroyed any hope of their being together.

Tears gathered in Nance's eyes, and she glared in bold accusation. Cory Miller had no feelings. He was a selfish beast. He wanted a pretty doll, a Krystal Adkins with bouffy-hair, a big chest, and a one-track brain. He wanted someone Nance could never be. Her love alone wasn't good enough, would never be good enough.

She couldn't find it in her heart to forgive him for it.

"What do you want me to say, Boo?" he released her hair and stared down at her. "What will make things right?"

He could talk all he wanted, but Nance had no intention of listening. No matter what he said, the words were too late.

Turning from him, she gestured to an empty lane, and then to Krystal and Sugar who were seated on the side bench, deep in a conversation. "It's your turn, Miller."

Cory stepped back and glanced over at Krystal and Sugar. Nance thought he would bowl his set, but instead, he took her arm.

"We're going to have this out right now, Nance Hadley."

"Let go of me!" Fierce anger threaded Nance's words.

"You want to cause a scene, Boo?" Cory grinned. "Go ahead. You want to embarrass yourself?"

Nance returned the smile with a saccharine grin. "I met a couple of real nice guys earlier, Cory. I'm sure they'd be happy to smash you to a pulp."

"You're doing a pretty good job of that all by your lonesome."

Nance had no reply. Cory didn't wait for one.

Grim with purpose, he pulled her over to Krystal and Sugar. "Guys, let's take a rain check on the game. Nance and I have some things to work out."

"Not to mention that you were going to wipe the floor with us," Nance added, trying to put a better face on disaster.

"Not to mention that." Cory's grin was easy.

Sugar looked at Nance and she knew that she need only say the word and he would defend her. But Cory was right. The problems between them would never go away until they talked it over.

Nance gave Sugar a brief smile.

He nodded. "Yeah. We're not up for bowling tonight, either."

Hoping that Krystal was having better luck than she was, Nance tried to catch Krystal's eye, but Krystal turned away. Nance thought she caught the suspicious glint of tears on Krystal's lashes.

It was clear that their plan, their perfect makeover plan, had failed.

CHAPTER FOURTEEN

Cory insisted on driving Nance's car. His long, programmer's fingers gripped the steering wheel so tightly, his knuckles showed red and white.

They sped through the night bathed in a tension-fraught silence, the hot breeze of a waning summer far too heavy to provide relief against the weighted air inside the convertible.

Although the trip was short, it seemed forever before Cory pulled into the circular drive of Nance's home. He allowed the car to idle for a moment before turning off the ignition. He didn't move, instead, he remained in the driver's seat, face forward, shoulders slumped.

"I picked up 'My Best Friend's Wedding,'" Nance said, a faltering attempt to fill the space between them. "Want to watch it with me? Julia Roberts plays the lead role."

Cory's answering laugh was devoid of humor. "I'm over my Tinker Bell phase."

"Does that mean you're over Julia Roberts too?" Nance opened the passenger-side door and hopped out of the car. "She's going to be devastated."

Cory looked at her then, his eyes so full of sorrow, that Nance was taken aback. "It won't be the first time I've hurt a woman," he said.

"Nor the last, no doubt." The flippancy of nance's reply was too tinged with bitterness to be taken as light-hearted. "C'mon, cory. I'll microwave some popcorn. It'll be like old times."

Cory nodded. Alighting from the car, he followed Nance into the house, switching on the lights as they passed. They stopped in the kitchen. Nance could see that Cory was remembering the last time he'd been there, just like she was.

The view of the lake was obscured by darkness, but Nance could hear the rush of water against the pebbled shore. The sound calmed her and gave her hope.

Surely, she and Cory could work things out. They'd been friends for such a long time. Surely they could go back to the way things were. It wasn't an unreasonable desire.

"You still buy those bottled cream sodas I like?" Cory asked. Nance's spirits lifted just a bit.

A LIFETIME LOVING YOU 253

This was normal. She hadn't realized how much she missed having Cory around.

"You're in luck." Her smile was impudent. "I like them, too."

Cory went to the refrigerator and stuck his head in. He came out with ham, cheese, mayonnaise, and a gourmet cream soda. From the pantry he pulled out a loaf of sourdough bread.

"Panera's Bakery," Nance told him.

"That's my Boo," Cory gave her a cheeky grin that sent her traitorous heart soaring. "Mind if I make myself a sandwich?"

"It's a little late for asking, don't 'cha think?" Nance pointed to the mayonnaise jar. Cory had already removed the lid.

Cory didn't look up from his sandwich. "You would not believe how hungry I've been since you kicked me out of your life."

In the midst of programming the microwave for popcorn, Nance froze. "I did not kick you out of my life," she said distinctly. "You made a choice. Am I supposed to feel sorry for you?"

Cory slathered a heaping spoonful of mayonnaise on the sourdough bread. "You could try." His tone was too nonchalant. Briefly, he glanced up at her, but Nance was stunned by the intensity in his gaze. Suddenly, she was gripped by the certainty that although Cory appeared to be focused on making a sandwich, he was leading her along a path of his choosing.

Nance had no answer for him, and the beeping of the microwave rescued her from having to say anything. She pulled the popcorn from the microwave and poured it into a bowl.

Placing the bowl near Cory's rapidly growing sandwich, she said, "I'm going upstairs to change. I'll be back in a minute." Then she escaped.

Ten minutes later, she returned wearing a pair of Old Navy sweat pants and a ratty T-shirt that she'd scrounged from the bottom of her drawer. Coming downstairs, she found Cory in the media room. He was already set up before the television, his sandwich half-eaten, and the majority of the popcorn gone. Nance snatched up the bowl and peered inside.

"You could have saved some, Cor." She popped a piece in her mouth.

"What? And ruin my image as a jerk?" Cory's roguish grin was so endearingly familiar that Nance couldn't help but return the smile.

"I'll make more." She hurried to the kitchen, all the while wondering who she was trying to fool. The change of clothes, the popcorn, the movie, they were all excuses. She didn't want to face the problems between Cory and her.

The best thing, she decided, was to forget this whole Krystal thing and go back to being friends. Cory would never have to worry about Nance hitting on him, she was done with that. No doubt their friendship would be all the better from this point on.

The popcorn was done after a few minutes. She returned to the media room with a full bowl and her own bottle of crème soda.

"I put the movie in," Cory said.

Nance placed the popcorn in the center of the table and settled onto the opposite end of the sofa from Cory.

"Thanks."

As the overhead lights began dimming, Nance glanced sharply at Cory. He had the dimmer in his hand. "We can watch with the light on," Nance pointed out.

"What's the purpose of THX sound and high definition television if you're watching with the lights on?"

"Beats me," Nance replied. "You're the one who chose this system. As far as I can tell it looks the same, and the sound is only ten times louder."

"Technology is wasted on you, Nance Hadley."

"You're absolutely right, Miller. And you know what? I don't care. I'm happy being me."

Cory tossed the dimmer onto the side table, leaving the room in semi-darkness. With a sigh, he dropped his head back on the sofa. "I said the wrong thing again, didn't I?"

"What are you talking about?"

"You know what I'm talking about." He lifted his head and looked at her. "I've been saying the wrong thing all night long."

Nance grabbed the popcorn bowl and held it before her like a shield. "Whatever."

"Not whatever, Boo. You're worth more to me than whatever."

Surprised, Nance could only stare at him, her heart aching for him even though her brain replied with a laundry list of reasons why a relationship between them would never work.

"Our friendship is important to me too," she answered carefully.

Disappointment in his eyes, Cory merely stared at her.

Nance couldn't hold his gaze. What if he saw how weak she felt? What if he saw how much she wanted him to touch her? She couldn't allow that. She was a mass of vulnerability, and he held the key to her destruction.

"Maybe it's not you, Cory. Maybe it's me. Over the last several days, I've gotten to know Krystal, and I find that she's actually a nice girl, once you get past a few personality traits. I like her."

A dull flush tinged Cory's cheeks. Nance could see it even in the muted light. "She was never interested in me. I knew that, Nance. I knew it all along."

"I thought you were trying to change her attitude."

Cory shook his head. "I doubt I would have gone to such effort if I thought I could really change her mind. Sugar's the man for her. I hope things work out for them." There wasn't the slightest hint of disappointment in Cory's voice.

"I hope so too." Nance tugged on her upper lip with her teeth.

"And us?" Cory asked. In one smooth motion, he slid across the sofa, coming to stop a hair's breadth distance from Nance.

Nance lifted the bowl of popcorn between them. "There is no us," she said, her voice shaking. "There never has been. I've finally learned to live with that."

"Because of Sugar?"

Nance shook her head. "I like Sugar, but liking and loving are two different things."

"I always thought so. I'm not so sure anymore." Cory removed the bowl of popcorn from Nance's hands and set it on the floor. "Lets start over, Boo." Eyes intent, he moved even closer, his lips stopping a breath away from her own.

A tremor shook her. Desire for Cory's touch flared to an agony of need inside her. But at what cost? She reminded herself as he came nearer. Then he was kissing her.

His lips brushed hers, feather-light, washed with an intoxicating sweetness that made her want more, deeper. And now, she was drowning in desire, hungry for more of his touch.

She wound her arms around Cory's neck, pulling him to her, tongue washing across his lips, and meshing together with his tongue, tasting the mingled flavors of popcorn butter and vanilla from the crème soda, along with that flavor that was all warmth and strength and Cory Miller.

He rained kisses across her face, down her throat, his hands roamed her, sending shivers of delight throughout her entire body.

She'd never known sensations like the ones that wrapped around her, teasing her, tantalizing her, whispering to her to forget everything, to let go of the past and give in to desire.

Nothing mattered but sensation.

Nothing was important except that at last, at long last, Nance had this chance, this one opportunity to be with Cory, to share her love with him.

It felt so good. So good as his hand skimmed her arm and moved up, bracing the back of her neck, and then slipped down, light-fingered to ease beneath her shirt and along the thin line of her abdomen.

"No," she whispered as his hand trailed up. The word was dragged from her, from some deep reservoir, a moral compass, that sent a trilling alarm warning that this wasn't what she wanted from Cory.

She wanted more. She had to remember that she wanted more.

"Nance," Cory breathed her name against her mouth, but his hand stilled.

Caught together in a moment where time moved with heartbreaking slowness, Nance pictured herself with painful clarity, head thrown back, lips parted, back arched, almost completely lost to reason, except for that nagging voice, so small as to be insignificant.

She didn't have to listen.

Cory was there. They were together. Couldn't they share this one moment of passion?

But it wasn't real. No matter how much she wanted this, no matter how much she wanted him, it wasn't real. A wave of remorse swept over Nance. The passion that had stolen reason ebbed, plunging her instead into a despair so great, she released a broken sob before she could stop herself.

"Boo?" Cory drew back. Gently cupping her face in his hands, he asked, "What's wrong, love?"

"I can't do this," Nance told him. Tears left itchy tracks down her cheeks.

Cory pulled her against him, wrapping her in the warmth of his strong arms. "It's okay, sweetie. We don't have to do anything you don't want to do."

"But I do want to," Nance hiccuped sorrowfully. "I just can't."

"Because of Krystal?"

Nance shook her head. "Not just because of Krystal."

"Why, then?"

"Because of everything."

"Help me understand, Boo." Cory ran a hand through his hair. "Please. Don't you know that it's you I want. For the last week, you've been playing keep away. You say you're letting go, but why? I thought you wanted us to be together."

"I do. I did," Nance tried to find the words to explain her feelings. "I had this dumb belief that if I loved you enough, somehow that would cover both of us." She gazed into his desire-filled eyes, her gaze tracing his passionate mouth.

"I wanted this, Cory. I did. I wanted for us to be one in heart and body."

Cory took her hand, his eyes fixed on hers with an unnerving intensity. "We can have that, Nance."

He lifted her wrist to his lips and kissed the tender skin on the inside of her hand, the motion rekindled desire in Nance.

She resisted. "No, Cory. I want more from you. I want commitment. And I want you to love me, not because of my looks, but because of who I am, and what we are together."

"You think I don't?"

"I know you don't."

"That's where you're wrong, Boo." Cory released her arm, his expression one of frustration. "You've been so wrapped up in being mad at me, and setting yourself up as a martyr, that you can't see how much I love you." Still gentle, he put her away from him and rose from the sofa. When he spoke, his voice was heavy with resignation. "This isn't really about appearances. It's not about

Krystal. It's not even about the past. It's about you not forgiving me for being an idiot."

"That's not true!" Nance denied hotly, passion transforming within the space of a moment into cold fear.

"Oh, it's true. On one hand, you say you want me, but now that I've got my head on straight, you're pushing me away."

"I'd be a fool to let you into my life, Cory. You've never done anything but hurt me."

"I'm sorry. I was an idiot. How many times do you want me to say it, Nance? How many ways? Is it something I'll have to say every day for the rest of my life? Or will you grant me leniency and only require that I save my groveling for Sunday penance?"

Nance wrapped her arms around herself. "You're being a jerk."

"You better believe it," Cory agreed. "I'm fighting for the woman I love. Do you hear me, Nance? I love you."

"You humiliated me," Nance returned. "That's not love. Now you don't have anything better to do, so you trying to hop into my bed. No, Cory. I'm not buying your line this time. And if you call me 'Boo,' I swear I'll sock you."

Cory was just as angry as Nance. "I was

scared. I did dumb things. But, my wanting you is not even remotely related to boredom."

"Oh? You forget, I was there, I saw how you drooled all over the shoes for Krystal. I refuse to be her stand-in."

Cory stared at Nance, anger warring with sadness and frustration on his handsome features. He opened his mouth once to speak and then, deciding against it, stomped from the room without another word. Moments later, Nance heard the front door open and slam shut and then the motor on her car roared to life.

The engine revved, followed by the screech of tires, and then silence.

Cory was gone.

And this time, Nance knew, there was no way to get back to before.

CHAPTER FIFTEEN

She had destroyed her life. With her own two hands, she'd taken her last chance at happiness and smashed it into a million pieces.

Nance lay as still as death at the center of her bed, her face leeched of color, the whiteness of her face accentuated by the gray, Egyptian-silk coverlet beneath her.

Her heart seemed caught, a fly encased and trembling in a web, hung in suspended animation and haunted by surroundings that reminded her of what she'd thrown away.

Foolish with hopes, she had decorated her bedroom with Cory in mind. The gray coverlet, because he hated Laura Ashley and anything with flowers on it. Then there was the giant, silver maple armoire and the four-poster bed with turned columns made from the same wood—Cory had pointed those out to Nance in a designer's catalogue she'd shown him when she was choosing a bedroom suite.

The John Hein table between the two armchairs in the sitting area was also chosen by Cory, an affectation that had set Nance back to the tune of ten grand.

It wasn't that Nance didn't like the furnishings. She loved them. In fact, Cory's taste was so closely aligned with her own that he possessed an almost uncanny perception of what she would have chosen on her own. Yet, they had chosen all of the items together.

Nance turned her head to one side, eyes touching on the French doors that led to the adjoining upstairs office—another living feature designed with Cory in mind.

The entire home was infused with Cory's spirit, a spirit she had invited, had found comfort in as she waited for him to realize that he loved her in return. Now, with their relationship in tatters, the room seemed to mock her.

Like heat, pain flashed in Nance's skull, and though she'd believed herself incapable of producing more tears, she found that she, indeed, could cry. She buried her face in her pillow, allowing the tears to fall, knowing she couldn't fight the heartbreak any longer, and wondering why she had tried.

Maybe Cory was right. She'd wanted him out of her heart because the pain of his choosing Krystal over her had been almost too much to bear.

And now, she was filled with too much anger and hurt and distrust to even care that his feelings for her had changed.

How could she forgive him when the hurt was deeper than she could ever have imagined?

He'd admitted his mistake. But it wasn't enough.

And there it was—like a flash of light going off behind closed eyes, Nance realized that, in part, the true reason she'd found it so hard to forgive Cory was that he'd gone to great effort to win Krystal's favor. And yet, with Nance, he'd done nothing more than send a few days' worth of flowers and an apology between passionate kisses.

Cory knew Nance loved him, he knew that he didn't have to make any effort to impress her. His lack of effort seemed an insult.

After all she'd been through for him, the very least he could have done was to get down on his hands and knees in the Corance cafeteria at lunchtime and grovel a bit.

No. That wasn't asking for too much. A billboard ad on Interstate 494 or a sky-written declaration above the state capital would work as well.

But, anything less than all-out, obvious commitment was unacceptable. Nance needed to forget that she'd been a consolation prize, accepted in part because she had curves in the right places.

Anything less, and she would feel that twenty-two years of devotion had gone far too cheaply. With trembling fingers, Nance reached over to trace a circle in the pillow beside her.

Lofty principles were of little comfort against the ache of desire and loneliness, but no matter how out-dated and seemingly restrictive, her principles were important to her.

Cory had to love her for who she was.

He had to see her as a valuable human being.

And, he had to respect that she'd waited more than twenty years for him to love her—she wanted their first time together to occur after the wedding. She'd always dreamed of the two of them coming together in an explosion of heat and passion, with no morning-after awkwardness. She wanted him to stay the entire night and every night and day thereafter until death parted them.

You're just afraid he'll change his mind if you give in. The thought was disconcerting, more so because it held a grain of truth. No matter how much she longed for Cory's touch, a one-night stand would destroy her.

A sound, like the spattering of gravel on glass, roused Nance from her despondency. She sat up on the bed, head to one side, listening. The sound came again, followed by several loud thumps and then a tap on the side window by the fireplace.

An intruder. That was the last thing she needed right now. Nance snatched the phone from its cradle beside the bed and quickly dialed 9-1-1.

"Emergency Services." The dispatcher's voice crackled over the line.

The tapping sound came again, louder this time.

"Someone's trying to break into my house," Nance whispered into the phone.

"Your address?"

"525 Canyon Center Road."

"We'll send a patrol car."

The tapping was even louder now, as if the intruder wanted her to know that he was coming for her. Shaking so hard she could hear her teeth chattering, Nance told the operator, "I'm going to put the phone down."

She laid the phone on the bed and looked around for a weapon. Who knew how long it would take for the police to arrive.

If she was going to be attacked, she was going to go down fighting.

The only readily available weapon Nance could locate was that Tess Gerritsen book she'd never had the chance to read.

She snatched it up, holding it before her as she crept over to examine the window.

Fear weighing her movements, she pulled aside the curtains and peeked out the window straight into the face of Sugar Smith.

"Sugar!" Nance squealed, relief spreading through her.

She turned the locks and pulled up on the sash. "What in the world are you doing...?" The question faltered on her lips as she took in Sugar's appearance.

He was dressed outrageously. Rather than answer her question, he crawled in through the window, and into the sphere of light that came from the bedside lamps. In the lighted room, Nance could see that Sugar's outfit was truly ridiculous.

He wore a pair of scuffed flat-leather boots with fold-over tops, and a pair of yellow- and lime-green-striped, form-fitting pants below a white-bloused shirt. The entire ensemble was set off by a bright-red scarf and a plumed hat.

Nance couldn't help herself—the fear, the relief, and Sugar's appearance conspired together causing her to burst into laughter.

"Are you recruiting for 'Delusions R Us,' or what?" Nance laughed.

Sugar responded with a solemn gaze. He took the book from Nance's hand and placed it on the Hein table. Taking her hand, he went down on one knee.

"Do not laugh at my attire, fair one. I have come on a quest."

"A quest?" Nance's shoulders shook with suppressed merriment, but Sugar remained serious. After a moment, Nance forced herself to calm down. "What kind of quest?" she asked.

"A quest of love." Sugar gazed up at her, humor lurked in the depth of his brown eyes.

"Oh really?" Nance inquired. "And what quest of love is this, Sugar?"

"This is no game, fair one." Sugar released her hand and reached into his shirt to remove a sheet of paper from which he began to read.

"Lovely Roxanne, you are the sun. You are the silver moonlight streaming through the trees. Have a care for my worn soul. I have been a fool. I beg of you, allow me to show you my true heart."

Nance was struck by a sudden concern. She and Sugar had already discussed their relationship. They'd already agreed to be nothing more than friends.

What was he trying to accomplish?

"We've been through this—" Nance started, but Sugar held up his hand.

"Do not speak, fair Roxanne. Ah, but wait." He searched about in his shirt once more. "How can I seek thy hand so improperly?" From his shirt, he retrieved a long, rubber object with an elastic band attached. He drew the band over his head and Nance could see now that the object was a fake nose—except that it was long, like Pinocchio's, or....

As Sugar continued, Nance caught her breath in surprise. "Allow me to introduce myself. I am Cyrano. I come to speak to you on behalf of my dear friend, Christian."

It all fell into place now.

"Cory sent you?" Nance's hand fluttered up to her throat.

"Christian," Sugar corrected. "He is tongue-tied and cloddish in the turning of a phrase. I am come merely as his humble emissary."

"I see," Nance said slowly, but she didn't see, not at all.

What was going on?

Did it matter?

Did anything matter except that Cory still

loved her, and he loved her enough to make a fool out of, if not himself, Sugar.

"As Christian's emissary," Sugar spoke solemnly, "I am delighted to extol your virtues, fair one. There is no other as fair as you, in young Christian's mind. In his eyes, you are a flower, a spring lily whose beauty can never fade, never wither, because it is a beauty that comes from the heart."

Nance looked behind Sugar, expecting Cory to jump out from behind him, or possibly from Sugar's carry-all shirt.

"Is that the message?"

"One thing more, fair Roxanne. Christian begs that you allow him to make his petition in person."

At that moment, the doorbell rang. Amazing. They had the speech timed to perfection. Wonderingly, Nance led Sugar from the room.

"Cory Miller!" She exclaimed as she threw open the door.

Cory stood framed in the doorway, one hand holding a champagne bottle and two crystal champagne flutes, the other hand, in the vise-lock hold of a police officer, gripped a lavish bouquet of roses.

After a moment of stunned silence as the police officer took in the picture Sugar made in his Cyrano get-up, the officer turned to Nance saying, "We had a call from a female saying that someone was trying to break in. I found this guy hiding out next to the bedroom window."

"It's just a joke, Officer," Cory said, turning pleading eyes to Nance. "Tell him, Nance."

"Nance?" she queried with a mischievous smile, "My name is Roxanne, and as for this prowler..." she paused, savoring Cory's suspense. No doubt he could see the headline in the *Pioneer Press*, CEO of Woodbury technology firm nabbed stalking partner. "This is Christian," she said finally.

The officer frowned. "From our information, this home is occupied by a Nance Hadley."

"That's right, officer."

"And is Miss Hadley in?"

"I'm she."

"But you said..." The officer stopped, looked them over once more, and with a sigh, released Cory's arm. "Doesn't matter." He pointed at Cory, "You're too old to be picked up for playing practical jokes."

"Yes sir." Cory was a meek as a lamb.

The officer cast a final curious glance at the group of them and then stalked off into the night, clearly not at satisfied with their answers, nor by the laughter that accompanied him to his patrol car.

"What is going on?" Nance asked when she finally gained control of herself.

Cory slipped inside and shut the door behind him. "I flubbed my part again."

"Maybe we should change your title from CEO to CEF, Chief Executive Flubber," Nance smiled to show she was just joking.

"Maybe." Cory thrust the flowers at her and then turned to Sugar and extended his hand. "Thanks for your help, Sugar. You're the best."

"Believe me, you could use the help." Sugar pulled the nose up, leaving it perched atop his head like some long, rubber horn with nostrils.

"I think I can take it from here."

Sugar nodded and reached for the door.

"Sugar," Nance spoke quickly. "What about Krystal? Is she... are you guys okay?"

Sugar smiled. "Wedding's set for a month from now."

Nance reached out, placing her hand on his arm. "I'm so glad for you Sugar. Krystal really loves you."

"Yeah, I know that."

"She's a forever kind of girl."

Sugar's eyes softened. "She's my forever kind of girl." He chucked Nance on the chin. "But, that doesn't mean you won't always have a place in my heart, Spike."

"Spike?"

"That's Krystal's new name for you."

Nance laughed. "Tell her I said I love it, and congratulations."

Sugar nodded. "I'll do that. Good luck." His gaze encompassed them both. He gave one final wave and then left them.

Nance locked the door after him and turned to face Cory, her heart beating in triple time.

"That's some joke, Miller."

Cory flashed his most endearing smile, but after a moment it faltered. Taking Nance's hand, he led her from the foyer to the living room. Leaving the champagne bottle and the two flutes on the coffee table, he took both of Nance's hands into his and drew her to rest against him, offering comfort, or drawing comfort, Nance wasn't sure which.

"I need you, Nance," he told her, his voice low and pleading. "Please don't let my foolish behavior stand between us." He bent his head and kissed the top of her ear, his warm breath sending shivers of delight along her spine.

"I don't want to be a consolation prize," Nance looked up at him and found herself drowning in the depths of blue eyes.

There was no escaping her feelings for Cory, she realized. Whether they were together or apart, she would always love him.

"There's no way you're a consolation prize, Boo. I'm the one. I couldn't see the beautiful woman right in front of me."

Nance stiffened at his words, causing his grip to tighten around her waist.

"Please, Boo, listen. To me, you are beautiful. Your spirit is beautiful. Your heart is beautiful. I can't live without you, without your beautiful heart and soul and spirit. You're everything to me."

"How long, Cory?" Nance asked, allowing herself to relax just a little. "How long will you believe all that?"

Cory placed a tender kiss on the right side of her pouty lips. "Until you stop fighting for the underdog." He kissed the left side of her mouth. "Until you stop giving of yourself."

He kissed her chin. "Until you stop loving a fool like me, Nance Hadley." He drew back so that he could look into her eyes, his gaze caressing her features with a thoroughness that was proof in itself of his sincerity. "I've been afraid. I've been a fool. But no more."

He slipped his hand into his pocket and withdrew a jeweler's box which he flipped open to reveal a breathtaking diamond ring.

"I've waited twenty-two years too long to ask you this question, Nance Hadley," he said. "I refuse to waste another moment. Please, will you marry me?"

Her eyes overflowing with love and tears of joy, Nance Hadley flung her arms around Cory's neck, because the answer was an unequivocal yes.

Cadeau Moments
Proudly Presents

& After
Mechelle Avey

coming soon from Cadeau Moments

The following is a preview of *& After*...

Dexter Stuart was a lunatic. Had to be. Only a lunatic would wear a wool overcoat in ninety-eight degrees of soup-hot, mosquito-swamp weather. Resolute, in spite of the heat, he sucked in a breath of the stifling air and tugged his purple Minnesota Vikings baseball cap down so that it sat low on his forehead, shielding his face.

He forced himself from his Mercedes, cursing the distinctive license plate that read "GEEK" in bold letters like a flashing advertisement of his presence. He should have brought the Lexus, but he'd forgotten about the plates.

It was too late now.

A quick glance about proved more habit than help. He couldn't see any futher than a foot in front of him because, as he now recalled, he'd substituted his prescription glasses for a pair of concealing shades. Nevertheless, at 6:00a.m. on a Saturday morning, surely the park was deserted.

Too late to bother about that one, as well. He should have chosen a better location for this meeting. Edgewater Park was only a stone's throw from his home in Woodbury, Minnesota's upper-crust Wedgewood community.

All Dexter needed was to run into some early bird neighbor, out for a walk or a jog, and his humiliation would be complete.

He patted his coat pocket, encountered the bulk made by his glasses, and gained a measure of comfort.

With sweat rolling down his back like a torrential rain storm, his effort to avoid being recognized seemed, in the clear light of an already sweltering morning, less than brilliant. In fact, as Dexter shuffled forward, his head down in an effort to appear innocuous, he had to wonder just what he'd been thinking in the first place.

Like a huge overcoat matched with a purple Vikes cap looked inconspicuous. Good grief, he was a flashing neon sign that read: "Boob Alert!"

He needed to peel himself from the smothering embrace of the coat, get rid of the cap, and. . . .

"Oof!" He tripped and landed in a heap on the sidewalk. The force of the impact knocked his sunglasses off, the plastic cracking apart against the hot pavement.

And—finishing his thought from earlier—he needed to put on his glasses so that he could see where the heck he was going.

Too late a third time. Quick steps approached him, followed by a woman's concerned voice asking, "Are you alright?"

Dexter rolled over. He squinted at the blurred countenance hovering above him. A hand, presumably for the purpose of aiding him in rising, appeared directly in front of his eyes. Embarrassment transformed Dexter's skin from heat-flushed to fiery red. Ignoring the woman's offer of assistance, he hoisted himself from the ground, maintaining a chagrined silence.

Great way to make an entrance. If he were a different person, he'd laugh the whole thing off, make some light-hearted quip, smooth things over. Unfortunately, he wasn't a different person. He was Dexter Stuart, and Dexter Stuart was so tongue-tied around women, he'd be better off with a giant paper sack stuck over his head than attempting to trade glib banter.

He forced himself to look at the blur.

"I'm fine," he told her. His tone was edged with a gruff irritation which only served to make him feel worse. First he'd played the buffoon, now he was shifting into jerk mode.

If this were a business deal, his next step would be simply to get the upper hand. Right now, the woman had all the advantage. He'd made too many mistakes—the idiot disguise, the trip-over-his-own-two-feet—heck, he couldn't even see her expression clearly. Her expression would have told him what she was thinking, how badly he'd come across. No doubt it was all she could do to keep from laughing her head off.

Fine.

Let her laugh. He was used to being the butt of jokes.

At least, he had been in the past.

That was the problem. Somehow, Dexter was allowing the past to affect his present. The past was the past, although it had played a role in motivating him to set this meeting. Nevertheless, in spite of the absurdity of the situation, there had been no hint of humor in the woman's lyric tone when she'd spoken to him.

It was time, Dexter decided, for his foolishness to end. Maybe he didn't have enough savoir-faire to rescue his ragged ego from embarrassment, but he could certainly put a halt to his run-away idiocy.

Self-reproach weighting his shoulders down, Dexter removed the heavy overcoat, pausing only to reach into his pocket and retrieve his prescription glasses. Coke-bottle thick, they were unharmed by his fall. He slipped them on, and the world righted itself, swinging from blurred incomprehensibility to sharp focus in the space of a single moment.

Dexter looked about quickly. The park was, as he'd suspected, deserted, except for the two of them.

He turned back to the woman. "You're Addison Bryant." He didn't bother making the statement a question.

She nodded, and, to her credit, she didn't appear as though she wanted to laugh—not that Dexter gave her more than a cursory perusal. One brief glance was enough to tell him all he needed to know.

Suddenly, Dexter found himself taken with an almost painful desire for her features to fade back to the fuzzed blur of moments earlier because Addison Bryant was beautiful— more than beautiful, she was stunning.

He'd known, of course, that she was a former model, but even so, he wasn't prepared for the peach fresh complexion over a heart face. Her lips were full and appeared to curve easily into a smile. Long, dark brown hair was pulled back in a clasp at the nape of her neck. Her blue eyes were large and luminescent. She was dressed smartly in a crisp, black pantsuit, and somehow, she managed to look fresh and cool, in spite of the heat.

In fact, Addison Bryant had the appearance of someone who'd never once broken a sweat. Dexter stooped to retrieve the damaged sunglasses. He couldn't help but wonder what she was thinking, how she saw him.

Not that it mattered. He rose, his heart filled with a sad resignation. No doubt to her, he was nothing more than a foolish man chasing a frivolous dream. His actions were indicative of a desperation that had little to do with logic and everything to do with bolstering his own vanity.

Lunatic, indeed. Addison Bryant couldn't help him. She couldn't understand his need to seek her out. How could she? How could anyone as lovely as the woman gazing at him understand the ravages his nerd heart had withstood?

"You're not hurt, are you?" she asked after the silence between them became uncomfortable. Her smile of concern was dazzling enough that Dexter felt a slight catch somewhere deep in his chest—more foolishness, something he could ill-afford.

"I'm fine," he told her.

Addison stuck out her hand again, this time in greeting.

Dexter took it, but he felt paralyzed. Nerves conspired with the heat to create damp circles under his arms. He saw her glance at the wet rings. He clamped his arms down tight and wished he possessed the strength to withstand the oven-like temperature of the coat.

"I don't think. . . ." Dexter stopped, his expression grim as he sought the words to end the meeting.

But what could he say? Irritation washed over him. Why did he even have to speak the words?

It was obvious they were wasting their time. Surely she could see that as well as he.

Heaven help him, what in the world had he been thinking? The meeting, the attempt at disguise both were exercises in self-deception. As a businessman in the cut-throat world of software development, Dexter understood, far too well, that he could not afford the luxury of even one moment's worth of self-deception.

"Look, Ms. Bryant—" he tried again.

"Call me Addison."

"Addison," Dexter amended. "This meeting was. . . ."

"A mistake?" she finished for him.

Relieved, he nodded. He'd begun to think he might have to convince her otherwise. After all, if he walked away, he'd be taking a hefty commission with him. Even so, Dexter couldn't help but think that in spite of the fact that his face appeared frequently in business journals and as an expert on television programs, Addison Bryant had expected better than the reality.

Dexter ignored the painful disappointment that nudged at him. He already knew he was no winner in the looks department.

He was what he was.

A geek. A social misfit whose genius in understanding the intricacies of temperamental computer software had earned him a fortune many times over, but fortune, or not, no amount of money could achieve what he truly wanted—love, a wife, children, his own family.

Even Addison Bryant was telling him so. She was an image consultant, supposedly capable of creating miracles—at least, that's what her ad in the yellow pages seemed to indicate—but no matter how beautiful and classy she was, she couldn't help him. Understandable. After all, she needed something to work with. A sow's ear wasn't even remotely close to silk.

For his own ego's sake, Dexter reworded her statement. "An

exercise in bad judgement," he said.

"Because you're embarrassed?"

She was certainly direct. Dexter turned his gaze from her finely etched features to stare at the lake in the center of the park. Morning sun dappled the water, sending pin points of white light racing over the lake.

"I'm embarrassed," Dexter agreed after a long moment.

"I have a feeling that telling you not to be embarrassed would be a waste of time."

"After the last few moments, it would be," he told her.

She smiled, a crooked up-turning of one side of her mouth that made her appear a puckish fairy formed with unearthly beauty. Dexter caught his breath and held it, reminding himself that women like Addison Bryant weren't attracted to geeks, and if they were, it was a matter of money rather than true affection.

Her grin widened, beguiling him. Unwillingly, he returned the smile. Moments later, they were both laughing uncontrollably. The sound of their humor shattered the early morning quiet, and along with it, some of Dexter's defensiveness.

"Mr. Stuart, I know you must be feeling awkward about meeting with me," Addison spoke in the lull that followed the spontaneous humor. "Please don't be." She laid a light hand on his shoulder. She seemed unconscious of the contact, but Dexter felt as though he'd been branded.

He couldn't recall the last time he'd been touched by a woman. No, that wasn't quite true. Kismet Trent had touched him. Ten years ago, on graduation night, she'd come up to him after the commencement ceremony, her face flushed and excited. They talked a bit—she was one of the few students who had always been nice to Dexter. Before leaving him, she'd given him a quick hug, started to walk away, and then, surprising him, she rushed back, and with an expression of daring, she kissed him full on the lips.

Back then, Dexter Stuart had been too shy and too much of the nerd to follow up and find out what she'd intended with that kiss. Now, he regretted his fear. For ten years, he'd regretted it, but perhaps it wasn't too late.

"Please don't be embarrassed, Mr. Stuart." Addison's voice broke through his cluttered thoughts, gently urging him to speak.

"There's a reunion," Dexter found himself saying. His voice sounded strangled and anxious. He cleared his throat.

"High school?" she asked.

Dexter nodded and felt himself blush as Addison studied him, her blue eyes seeming to catalogue every feature, from his thick glasses to his square, determined jaw. He felt as though all of his thoughts and feelings were splashed in a banner across his face.

"There's nothing wrong with trying to find a sense of balance, Mr. Stuart." Her soft voice soothed away the last fragments of his unease.

"Balance has little to do with what I want," he felt compelled to point out.

Addison shook her head. "I disagree." Suddenly, without a word of warning, she moved away. Walking over to a dusty picnic table, she brushed it off and then sat on the wooden table top before beckoning for Dexter to join her.

After a brief moment of surprise, he followed her. As he approached, she patted the space beside her. He joined her, settling himself at a safe distance, wondering why he didn't just end the conversation.

The answer, he admitted to himself, was that he wanted to hear what she had to say. He needed to be sold that bill of goods, that dream that she could, indeed, turn him into a handsome prince.

But Addison Bryant wasn't talking about appearances. "Balance," she repeated, turning her face away from Dexter to watch a pair of Canadian geese settle into the water. "You're a very successful man, Mr. Stuart."

"Call me Dexter."

She nodded, as though she had achieved a goal of some kind. If she had, Dexter didn't know what it was. She lifted a single eyebrow in inquiry. "Dex for short?"

"That's fine," Dexter's tone was noncommittal, though inwardly, he felt a surge of pleasure. No one had ever called him Dex. He'd always been Dexter the geek, or worse—in high school—Dexter Pester.

"Success doesn't necessarily equal balance, Dex. You're consistently listed as one of the wealthiest men in the country, and yet, you're single. From what I've read, you don't even have a pet. You rarely take vacations, and when you do, they're working vacations. You've got success, Dex, but it's not balanced."

"You did your research," Dexter noted, feeling as if he'd just been sucker punched. Somehow, he'd gotten the impression that Addison Bryant was a fragile beauty, too delicate to even state her distaste for Dexter's clear lack of fashion sense. Now, he was beginning to wonder if her classic beauty hid the proverbial knife cloaked in velvet.

"I did my research," she agreed, her gaze moving in a probing sweep across his face. "From what I've read, you prefer straight shooters."

"I guess I do," He smiled, understanding now that she was trying to set the ground rules in line with what she thought he wanted. "What about you?"

"I can hold my own."

Dexter found himself relaxing a bit. Addison Bryant was beautiful, but there was also a brain inside that pretty head. He would be hard-pressed not to like her for her personality.

"Look, Addison, or should I call you Addy, for short?"

She grinned. "Addison. I hate Addy-for-short."

"Duly noted. Here's the straight line, I'm not looking for a guru, or a business coach. At this point, balance is the last thing on my list."

"What's first on your list?"

"I've been asked to present a speech in Wolf River, Kansas to one hundred of my former school mates, people who used to call me Dexter Pester, and Dorkman." He gave a rueful laugh. "I've talked to audiences ten times that size, but there's something about going home. . ." He looked at her, his expression intense. "I was the class geek. Valedictorian. Voted most likely to never kiss a girl." He studied her covertly, looking for pity. He didn't find any. Good. He hated pity.

He continued, "At the risk of being a jerk, these people don't want to celebrate me as the home-town hero made good. They're small-town. They want to gossip about how I still look like a dork."

He paused, almost expecting her to protest his assessment of his appearance. When she didn't, he went on. "I want advice on how to put myself together. I don't have to be Tom Cruise. Decent will do."

She nodded. "Anything else?"

Dexter started to shake his head, but her quiet intensity made him want to tell her everything. "There's a girl." He glanced at her to gauge her reaction to the statement. It was clear that she was listening, although she didn't look at him. Instead, she watched the geese, her profile to him. She appeared carved from gossamer, so lovely and fragile, far too beautiful for a nerd like him.

"Kismet Trent," he said, forcing himself to focus on the conversation at hand.

"From high school?"

Dexter nodded and turned his gaze to the birds. "I don't know how she felt... or rather, feels. We haven't stayed in touch."

"But you want to see if there's a chance?"

Dexter couldn't think of a response. How could he explain that he'd held on to hope for ten years. He was more of a fool than he'd realized.

A hesitant touch on his hand caused him to glance down in surprise. He met Addison's inquiring gaze. For a moment, he forgot that he was a nerd. He smiled at her, acquiescing to whatever it was that she wanted from him.

She took his large, finely-boned hand into her own, doing nothing more than holding it. Together, wrapped in the quiet of early morning, hands clasped in an easy hold, they watched the sun lift itself over the lake.

A sense of peace stole over Dexter, making him loathe to pull back, to break the bond that seemed to tie them together in a moment of exquisite beauty.

At last, Addison eased her hand from his. "I've done my research, Dex, but there was nothing in the papers about your heart."

"My heart?" Dexter couldn't hide his surprise.

"It's funny, you read about someone and you think you know them. But you don't, not really. I can't believe that I fell into that trap. I should know better. Dex, you've been honest with me, now I'm going to be honest with you."

Dexter met Addison's gaze. He was gripped with the certainty that he would not like what she was about to say. This was where she would tell him that she couldn't help him.

"I was wrong, Addison. I don't think our meeting was a mistake," Dex spoke quickly, the words tumbling from his lips with a frenetic quality.

"I don't think it was a mistake." She sounded surprised. "You should know, however, that I don't have a lot of clients. In fact, you're my first."

A feeling of relief washed over Dexter. "And you're afraid

you might ruin my fashion sense?" he laughed.

"It's not my intention to trick you, but everyone has to start somewhere."

"Your ad said you were a model."

"I was, for almost ten years. I started when I was seventeen."

"What type of modeling did you do?"

"A lot of print. Runway. Some trade, near the end."

"I see. Perhaps I should call another firm." Dexter was joking, but when he caught the glimpse of sorrow in Addison's eye, he quickly grew serious. "Look, Addision, I need help. I haven't the faintest idea what you mean by balance, but I do know that success can build a prison around a man making it almost impossible to get help when he needs it—especially when he needs the kind of help I need."

"I understand better than you know, Dex." Addison's eyes held a haunted look.

"Well, I couldn't care less how many clients you've had. And, I admit that I wasn't sure about this whole thing at first, but I don't want to be labeled a geek the rest of my life. I don't want to go back to Wolf River and have them whispering behind my back about how nerdy I am. I may be successful, but Dexter Pester lives on. Maybe I'm stupid to think changing my looks can change my life. I just don't want to wear the label someone else made for me."

In one swift motion, Addison Bryant leaned forward and placed a soft kiss on Dexter's lips. She sat back, smiling at his stunned expression. "I completely agree, Dex. Now we can drop that most likely to never kiss a girl label. It may not be your first kiss, but it won't be your last after I get through with you. You trust me, right Dex?"

Still reeling from Addison Bryant's precipitous kiss, Dexter nodded his head dumbly.

"Good," She leaped down from the picnic table and brushed the dust from her trousers. "I'll give you a call next week to schedule our first image session. Remember that you trust me. I won't let you down."

She raised her hand in an airy wave and then left him. He watched her get in her car and drive away. Dexter Stuart, the king of geeks was about to get a makeover, and he couldn't help but wonder what in the world he'd gotten himself into.

About the Author

Mechelle Avey is the author of four Cadeau Moment books.
She lives with her computer nerd husband and
two children in Minnesota.